BRUTAL
JUSTICE

BRUTAL JUSTICE

YOUR GUIDE TO BEING A VIOLENT VIGILANTE, CRIME-FIGHTING SUPERHERO

MARK SEWELL

iUniverse®

BRUTAL JUSTICE
Your Guide to Being a Violent Vigilante, Crime-fighting Superhero

iUniverse books may be ordered through booksellers or by contacting:

iUniverse
1663 Liberty Drive
Bloomington, IN 47403
www.iuniverse.com
1-800-Authors (1-800-288-4677)

ISBN: 978-1-4917-8933-9 (sc)
ISBN: 978-1-4917-8932-2 (hc)
ISBN: 978-1-4917-8934-6 (e)

Print information available on the last page.

iUniverse rev. date: 02/18/2016

Warning!

For Entertainment Purposes Only!

This is a work of fiction...that means it ain't real. Furthermore, the entire premise is a joke; that makes it double not real.

Beyond that, nothing in here is a good idea for stuff to do, so <u>DON'T FUCKING DO IT!!!</u>

If you are so amazingly stupid as to actually attempt anything contained in this book, it's your own fucking problem.

You have been warned.

The author takes no responsibility for your actions, nor any of the prison shower rapings such idiocy may result in.

TABLE OF CONTENTS

ACKNOWLEDGEMENTS

It is said that no man is an island.
Others have said that it takes a village to raise a child...guess they never heard of a single mother.

However, they all make the salient point that life is largely a team effort, and this applies to Justice endeavours as well (depending on your **Unique Hero Type** of course...more on that later). This book would have been completed without the assistance of others, but it would not have been nearly so awesome; many folks leant their efforts to creating a truly excellent end product.

So, without further ado, let's introduce you all to the ***Brutal Justice Entertainment Dream Team.***

- **Michael Reeve:** Photography, photo-wizardry, and apprentice vigilante.
- **Urban Knight:** Photography, and the other half of the Dynamic Duo.
- **David Wilcox:** Artist extraordinaire, responsible for the cover illustration, and bringing the ***Toxic Whale*** to glorious, horrific life.
- **Ashley Duguay** and **Rachel Gray:** Never has vigilante Justice looked so stylish.
- **Sergio Mazzotta:** No one else could better capture the vivacious, yet ready-for-ass-kicking attitude put forth by the stylish (yet deadly!) female superheroes. The pictures you see in the finished product cannot compare to the photo composition originally attained.
- **Karese (AKA The Destroyer):** My loving wife, who has been a true partner on the long, weird road of Justice...I don't know where life will take us always, but together we'll kick adversity in the face, and make it drink its own urine!

And finally, I must thank all the assholes, dick-faces, terrorists, murderers and assorted fucked-up, brain-dead, sadistically evil savages that deserve a jolly good shit-kicking; you made writing this easy.

PROLOGUE

So, you've decided to take up the vocation of being a ruthless vigilante, taking the law into your own hands, then twisting it into a pretzel and chucking it aside when it gets in the way. Well, I have one thing to say to you...

Good idea, man! Go for it!

But before you grab the nearest blunt object, wrap a scarf around your face and run off into the night, there are some things you must consider. Here are some of them; be honest with yourself.

- Are you able to beat up a MMA competitor, or does your previous level of conflict experience involve yelling at a Starbuck's employee over the level of foam on your cappuccino?
- Can you tell the difference between a revolver, an auto-loading pistol, a rifle or shotgun, and a pellet gun? More importantly, which should you choose for shooting a pedophile in the testicles while tied to a chair in your dungeon?
- Do you **have** a dungeon? If not, are you willing to build one within 90 days of commencing your righteous Crusade of brutality?
- What is your favourite colour?
- What does your power animal say about your crime-fighting style? Answer in 3-5 pages.
- Any thoughts as to a catchphrase or battle-cry (Screaming **"Save the whales!"** as you lay about you with a machete really throws people off)?
- Do you at least own a ski mask?

There are plenty of other concerns as well, like funding, plausible deniability, fitness, what performance enhancing drugs to take, etc. Fear not, bold adventurer, for I have the answers you <u>need</u>. I'll even coach you in the fine art of creating your very own mythology, turning disjointed jotting down of facts and rants into a masterful memoire anyone would be happy to read (and buy).

You've had your whole life to be normal, and what did that get you? Not much, or you wouldn't be reading this. So fill your lungs with a heroic breath, shout "Fuck You!" so loudly it resounds through the Halls of Valhalla, and leap into the void. Jump into my world, where adventure abounds and laws don't apply. Jump into a realm of... abnormality; it is your destiny. Take your place amongst those proud few with the strength of will to grapple the miscreants and pummel them into submission.

We have pizza. ☺

INTRODUCTION

Being a violent vigilante has long been a valued part of the beautiful tapestry which makes up society at large. In order for the vast majority of folks to remain happy in their safe little bubbles of innocence, like well-tended sheep, some force must counter the minority of folks who stalk them like hungry wolves. Part of this function has, of course, been performed by the military at a national level, and by the police forces at a provincial/state and city level, but they need help from outside the bounds of lawful society...they always have. Such a force sporadically appears, in an unforeseeable pattern of awakened folks who heed the call, out of a sense of duty, honour, rage, bitterness, or just sheer boredom.

This is where you come into the picture, bold reader. You are set to join the ranks of those who have borne a multitude of names throughout the ages, most commonly and coolly though, as vigilantes, crime-fighters...as superheroes.

That's right, you can rise to the ranks of those who usually are encoded in myth and fiction; by stepping outside the constraining structure of societal mores and "sanity", you access a realm of non-stop adventure and Justice (Justice is always capitalized...trust me, you'll understand why soon). But be warned, I'm not speaking about some hippy, pie-in-the-sky, visualize your best foot forward, imaginary adventure, fuck no! I'm talking alley stalking, leaping from rooftops, running from pursuing forces, car chasing, fence-hopping, baseball bat bashing, napalm burning in the night fun. You don't get spooked by bullets, do you?

This manual is here to guide you into your new life of adventure smoothly, answering practically any possible query you might have about starting up. Helpful tips will save you start-up cash, as well as hefty lawyer fees down the road. Time won't have been wasted learning stuff the hard way.

If you turn back now, your life is going to be the same as it has up to this point; safe, predictable, high likelihood of reaching retirement age, on the track to a 3 bedroom house, 1.8 kids and half a dog... boring as fuck. If you beckon the call though, life will never be dull. You may get shot, stabbed, clubbed, or blown up by a bomb...but you won't be bored! And if you do your job right, you'll be fine anyway, as all the people with motive to do such things will be dead. So relax already, you'll be okay...probably.

{CHAPTER ONE} THE DREAM

Let me present you a scenario:

A lone, masked figure sits perched upon a rooftop, keeping watch on the citizens below. They pass by down there, unaware of their silent protector keeping a vigilant eye out for danger, ready to leap into action at a moment's notice. All is quiet, other than the background noise of the city until...a scream is heard!

Ignoring all risk, the hero tosses a rope over the edge of the building, the untied end reaching to the ground far below. Taking a firm grip with his Gauntlets of Justice, he slides down at a break-neck pace, only slowing his descent as the pavement appears to rush up to meet him. Before his feet even make contact, he is leaping into action; he assessed the situation during the downwards journey, so the leader of the mugging scum is the first target.

Blam!!! *A thunderous right-cross pistons into the face of the scum-rot savage, crushing the nose and sending him to the ground in an insensate heap. With the first threat taken care of, only 5 thugs remain...child's play; they have no idea what magnitude of threat they are facing. ☺ Deploying the extendable baton with a threatening "Snick!", the paragon of Justice, this towering force for good, hurtles into their midst, laying all about himself in a beautiful ballet of pain and well deserved injury. The criminals never stood a chance, and they cannot even attempt to resist as their hands are zip tied together, interlocking with one another to make an easily identifiable, ungainly and immobile present for when the police arrive.*

The beautiful woman who has just narrowly averted defilement and injury through the swift actions of her savior shyly looks into the masked face, with eyes full of wonderment—awe even—and asks "Who are you? You have my eternal thanks, but can I at least know your name?" The hero looks deep into her eyes and says "You can call me **Savage Justice, Anonymous Protector of the Innocent**."

And with that, he turns his face into the night, racing off to see what other wrongs might be righted in the night-time corruption which plagues the city after dark.

Pretty great, yes? Come on, admit it, you have a scenario just like this pretty much in *your* head; only the number of criminals, the gender of the victim, and the height of the building are up for discussion. Well, I have a news flash for you...it usually goes a little something like this:

- "An unidentified moron plummeted to his death when the rope he was sliding down the side of a building with snapped in half; details at eleven."
- "A local man is in a coma, having been beaten half to death after attacking 6 men for no reason at all. He was wearing a mask and carrying weapons...police are calling it a clear cut case of self defense...charges are likely when he recovers."
- "A 29-year-old man was sentenced to 5 years prison time in connection with a savage beating last year, when he severely injured 6 men who were doing nothing to provoke the attack. During the trial his defense attorneys argued that he had been rushing to the aid of a woman that the men were trying to mug or sexually assault, but this mystery woman has never materialized."

So what gives? How did it go so wrong most of the time? Why didn't the heroic man of mystery get the fame and the girl? Why do so many potential vigilante superheroes end up dead, crippled or anally raped in prison? It is actually very, very simple, folks...they did not bother to think of what their unique hero type was. Your hero type will inform much of what you should do, how to do it, where to do it, and what equipment is required. Fear not though, brave reader, for you have this handy manual to guide you along the correct path.

{CHAPTER 2} WHAT HERO TYPE ARE YOU?

Not all heroes are the same; they have different motives, different strengths, different goals, and even different philosophies about how best to crush the criminal underclass into a sticky goo. Violent vigilantes are people, after all, with differing backgrounds and commitments. A soccer mom who volunteers with the PTA, for instance, will likely stalk the degenerate scum of society in a different fashion than a bachelor living in a run-down, inner city apartment. They each bring different things to the table; she likely has more disposable income for cool, high tech death devices, as well as a bitchin van, but he will have more free time, as well as easier access to crime...less travel time equals more clobbering time (heroics involves equations too). To apply a one-size-fits-all approach would neglect their unique talents, and ignore the crime-fighting opportunities inherent to their societal roles; she could target depraved perverts with rapist tendencies, using herself as bait, an approach which the unshaven bachelor will likely have very limited success with.

So, keeping these realities in mind, I shall present you with a sampling of different hero types, along with a few basic points to think about with each one. They are not exhaustive, and are meant to stimulate your imagination rather than lock you into any particular role. This ain't the army, son; you are free to explore many options, blending them until you come up with the perfect vengeance recipe, personalized to perfection.

Random Encounters: This refers to the free-form type of vigilante, who tends to go with what the universe provides as targets. Often viewed as lacking direction, he views himself as a balancing agent, one who is guided by random chance. Perhaps there will be a mugging in a parking lot at the grocery store; perhaps a rape will be attempted while he takes a piss at the bar...there are no mundane moments for this person. Plenty of foot patrols will be the order of the day; when not stuck in unavoidable commitments, get out there into the world! Adventure lies just beyond that door...or in that alley... or perhaps behind those bushes, etc. Randomly driving around the city side streets at night can be productive as well.

If this seems like you, always travel with an easy to put on mask, along with some cut-resistant gloves. You won't have time for full disguise; if you try for that, the miscreant will have already done their evil deed. Just mask up, pull some gloves on and jump into action. Get into the habit of seeing the escape routes around you in every situation, as the cops won't give you a medal for your efforts.

The Vengeful Detective: This hero type tends to be very focused and methodical; to them, the random approach is too much wasted time for not enough effect. Often burning with a cold rage, perhaps fueled by previous, personal trauma, the vengeful detective tends to focus mostly on certain crimes they find most heinous. Child molesters are a favourite target (as they should be), along with serial rapists, high level drug dealers, and serial murderers. Some may target corrupt cops and politicians also, but this is less common.

If you feel a deep resonance with this powerful archetype, you're not alone; Batman, Rorschach, and others of their ilk have long been fan favorites. You just make it real, and take it a tad further. You'll need to hone your research skills, and practice surveillance techniques as well. Hunting cameras set up in strategic places for staking out perps, directional microphones and glasses with built-in video recording capacity will be handy gadgets. A police scanner could be handy at times also...but what you really need are some computer hacking skills, and knowledge of how to mask your electronic presence.

Another great thing to do is imitate To Catch a Predator, and entrap pedophiles by posing as a kid seeking sex in order to lure them to your handy lair of death (that's another thing which you might add to the list of things to get: a *Lair of Death*). You will have the time to get into costume, put on disguises, and set up elaborate punishment schemes, so get creative with it!

4

Emotional Torture/Blackmail: This vengeance specialist is a connoisseur of emotional pain; they know that physical pain is over far too quick, and might let someone escape their punishment just as it was getting juicy. Although they don't directly inflict physical damage to the intended target, no one in their sights ever gets off lightly. Corrupt cops and politicians can fall victim to this hero type as easily as anyone else.

Do you ever wish to get revenge on the corporate bastards who foreclosed on that old lady's house? How about the jerks that got rich as they fucked everyone else by screwing the economy to death while floating along above the reach of the law? If you said yes, this might be your niche. The great thing about it is that the more they have to lose, the more easily they can be harmed. Make them explain to their wife why all that gay rape porn keeps coming to their house each month. How would they like explaining all the neo-Nazi propaganda which keeps getting forwarded to their boss, Mr. Goldstein, from their work e-mail account (note: requires hacking skills or the use of handy virus software)?

Or you can just keep mailing them dead rats in the mail, preferably with the return address of someone else you're targeting at the same time. Trust me, a constant parade of dead animals in the mail will do wonders for their state of mind.

Targeted Assassination: Never send a dead rat to do a bullet's job. This hero type is straight up violent vigilante all the way, but zeroed in on one target at a time. They may be a fan of eliminating only a certain sub-set of criminal, or their range might be quite varied; whatever the case, though, the important thing is that the target is dead, dead, **dead!** Suffering is irrelevant...eliminating the degenerate is paramount.

If this sounds enticing, great! You are in for a life of satisfaction at a job well done again and again, as the body count racks up along the way. You will need a few things though, such as a silenced bolt-action rifle with a scope, select close-quarters blunt trauma death devices, and other such things. A working knowledge of poisons (preparation and administration) will open doors, and you may find explosives handy as well. Develop disguise skills to blend in when heading to and from the area of operations.

Lucky for you, the media will assist greatly in target selection, as they love to blather on about various heinous criminal bastards, and tell where they're incarcerated as well as announcing their release dates. Between television and internet news, you will find a steady stream of assholes to blow away.

SWAT-Style Extreme Home Invasion: This dude does it pretty much exactly like it sounds, except that he does it solo (generally) rather than with a team for back-up. He finds out where the most notorious drug houses are, possibly from plainclothes hanging out in dive bars, the news, or by monitoring a police scanner. But once the target zone is decided upon, look out! No hint of caution or concern for self-preservation here, just balls-to-the-wall action following the reinforced door hitting the floor.

If you choose this option, damn, you are in for one wild ride! You may not live very long, but you sure will have lived...nothing gets the adrenaline coursing through one's veins like a barrage of gunfire from multiple directions all at once.

You get to exercise your creativity here, as there are a few different approaches to the same goal. You'll want to be armoured to the max, naturally, but do you want to look like SWAT, complete with insignia, or do you want to go for that fucking bat-shit crazy vibe? Why not throw a chicken suit over the armour, with a pink dildo dangling from a spring on your head? Either way should give a momentary advantage as the bad guys determine whether to shoot or not.

Bombs may help to increase your likelihood of survival...just think about it. ☺

The Parkour/Free-runner: Sheer physicality and perfection in motion are the game for this heroic individual. Fighting crime is almost secondary to him, as he leaps through the urban landscape like something which has popped straight from the pages of a comic book. Normally you'd need computer animation to see effects as spectacular as what gets done right before your eyes...Jackie Chan ain't got shit on our hero here, no sir. Whether it's leaping from a 6th floor balcony, ending with a forward roll and a kick in the face to a mugger, or simply sailing over a fence like a being freed from the bounds of Newtonian physics, this dude embodies speed, grace and agility, and looks good while doing it.

If you want this, turn off your computer and start getting in motion right now. You'll feel completely heroic and amazing sailing over an alley far below, leaping from rooftop to rooftop like a human sized squirrel. This is a great hero category to mix in when blending the various categories to arrive at your unique hero profile.

The High Tech Genius: This is exactly like it sounds; a genius who can go past the limits of most mortal beings by utilizing the immense power of the mind to create. At the lower limits, it involves the ability to create your own nervous system disruptor weaponry. At the highest levels, dude, you're Iron Man!

If you resonate with this category, well, please write a book of your own, because you're probably way smarter than me.

Your Own Unique Hero Style: This depends on you; no one can tell you what sort of violent vigilante you are deep down at the core. Through a process of introspection, visualization, and probably a few false starts, eventually a true identity will emerge, ready to take the world in a hail of bullets (if that turns out to be your thing).

But please don't feel constrained by the above categories; they are there only as guideposts, not as adamantium bars to cage you in. The list was not exhaustive, as to list every possible permutation would take a book published in several editions...and would bore everyone to death, including me. So go ahead, mix and match ideas from above, or throw them in the trash and construct an entirely new category that no one else could have possibly imagined! This is a journey of discovery and empowerment.

And if you cannot figure it out, well, fuck it, just move on to the next section! Perhaps what is needed will fall into place once you've settled on a name.

{CHAPTER 3} WHAT'S IN A NAME? A LOT, IT TURNS OUT...

Your name is a reflection of what sort of hero you intend to be, and it will affect media coverage as well if they find out about all the good works you're doing. A smart hero uses this to good effect, gaining the advantage by crafting a name the criminals will cringe in fear of every time the urge to sin arises in their rotten brains. Conversely, adopt a ridiculous name none will be able to fear, ever, and reap the rewards as scum and law enforcement alike underestimate and discount the danger posed by such a silly person. *"Another crack house blown up by **The Pink Kilt, Ravisher of Virgin Goats**...hmmph, sorry folks, but I can't say it with a straight face..."* decide what media response best serves the greater mission and run with it.

The proper name is also a totally awesome tool as regards self-perception. Psychological research shows that merely thinking of oneself as a superhero unlocks some of those traits (strength, stamina, confidence); this is a bonus you need, and it's completely fucking free! It also stacks on top of all other bonuses you get through training, exercise, etcetera, so there's zero risk. And it can be unlocked by a name.

Here's an example: *While waiting in line at the bank, you notice someone pull a gun at the cashier wicket; a robbery is now in progress. You don't have your body armour, and even if your disguise were available, there'd be no time to put it on (plus, you're already on camera anyway...). Confidence wanes, and you almost conform to the societal norm of being a fucking scared little sheep in the face of danger; baaaaa! But then, you remember who you are; the true, heroic identity rises from the depths, and a name, your true name bitch-slaps all fear aside. **"I am Crimson Death, Destroyer of Evil!"** No longer afraid, a mighty roar emerges from lips curled back in a vicious snarl, and the degenerate scum of a robber barely has time to register that* *things have changed before he screams, screams like an extra in a horror movie due to his broken arm flopping limply at his side. The gun falls harmlessly to the ground, as you nonchalantly step to the teller and put your card into the reader, entering the PIN and holding the sobbing robber in place with a booted foot on his neck; "I'd like to withdraw $75 from my checking account, please."*

Wow, pretty goddamned, motherfucking great, right? Damn, dude, you saved the day and looked good doing it too, all because of a name (and perhaps some martial arts combined with steroids...more on that later). I think you're getting the picture now, so let's look at some considerations which might help guide one to the perfect crime-fighting name.

- Perhaps you want to be a grim, Charles Bronson type of vigilante, gritty and dark; something along the lines of *Black Falcon, Dark Justice*, or *Crimson Death* might suffice.
- For the zany lunatic style of heroics, screaming something like *"Beware, fools, you face* **The Speckled Nematode, Glorious Celebrant of Mom's Basement!***"* can provide a momentary edge as evildoers are immobilized with laughter or confusion (bonus zaniness points if you bludgeon them to death with a huge rubber dildo).
- Or perhaps you tend to stick with a particular type of weapon for Justice Enforcement. For those heroes with a signature method of death dealing, a literally themed name can make great sense. For example, if your preference is to burn criminals to death with napalm when they least expect it, suitable names might include *Napalm Death; Burning Justice, Fiery Retribution*, or any other flame based name. *Flame Falcon, Bringer of Swift Vengeance*...you get the idea.

In a land of almost limitless choices, however, it can be difficult to narrow the options down, let alone decide upon just one. With this in mind, I have developed a handy decision making tool for new heroes to use. I present you with...**The Superhero Name Generator.**

There are five lists of words, handily numbered 1, 2, 3, 4 and 5. You simply take a word from list 1, and combine it with a word from list 2 in order to come up with your core name. You can use the word "The" before the first word if you wish (as in *The Swamp Being*, etc.). For some, the core name will be sufficient, with all the right connotations they are seeking. Hyphenations are optional.

For others though, the option to flesh it out with descriptors comes in next. A bonus descriptor from list 3 can be used, but isn't always needed (hence it being optional...duh). Then simply pick a word from list 4, and connect it with a word from list 5; connect those two words with "of" or "for" and a brand new superhero is born, with a pithy name as well. ☺

List 1) Sloth; Ultra; Ghost; Beast: Danger; Dark; Robo; Spider; Bat; Adventure; Tree; Master; Man; Swamp; Bionic; Crimson; Purple; Iron; Golden; Silver; Blood; Black; Mega; Vigilant; Steel; Amazing; Vigilante; Doctor; Night; Spirit; Captain; Lieutenant; King; General; Major; Eagle; Furious; Astonishing; Virtuous; Dangerous; Yellow; Orange; Pirate; Professor; Your nationality (Canadian, American, Russian, etc.); Justice; Lizard; Speckled; Moon; Solar; Death; Whale; Toxic

List 2) Man; Woman; Boy; Girl; Beast; Sentinel; Thing; Bot; Guardian; Star; Master; Avenger; Legend; Knight; Lotus; Fist; Warrior; Being; Pirate; Amazing; Justice; Owl; Eagle; Vengeance; Panda; Name of your country (Canada, Brazil, Russia, America, etc.) or your nationality (Canadian, American, Russian, etc.); Crusader; Justice; Platypus; Death; Nematode; Bolt; Whale

List 3) Mighty; Heroic; Dangerous; Vigilant; Vengeful; Furious; Astounding; Violent; Energetic; Brutal; Enthusiastic; Glorious; Bringer; Swift; Beautiful

List 4) Champion; Destroyer; Protector; Hunter; Defenestrator; Avenger; Upholder; Stalker; Accumulator; Paragon; Exemplar; Master; Lover; Butcher; Defender; Biter; Scourge; Fighter; Slayer; Vigilante; Harvester; Warrior; Apostle; Annihilator; Dispenser; Ravisher; Enemy; Seeker; Celebrant

List 5) Justice; Truth; Intoxication; Decency; Worms; Mimes; Laziness; Earth; Chaos; Knives; Virginity; Goats; Innocence; Adventure; Danger; Virtue; Forests; Knowledge; Freedom; Decay; Zombies; Villainy; Thugs; Goodness; Criminals/Crime; Evil; Demons; Death; Trees; Poverty; Spiders; Centipedes; Squirrels; Mom's Basement; Vengeance; Miscreants

Alrighty then, let's see what you can have, eh?

- ***Bionic Crusader, Brutal Stalker of Squirrels***
- ***Black Fist, Mighty Protector of Innocence***
- ***Black Pirate, Mighty Defenestrator for Freedom***
- ***Tree Warrior, Violent Hunter of Evil***
- ***Dark Guardian, Vigilant Master of Centipedes***
- ***Swamp Being, Vengeful Master of Knives***
- or the simple, elegant yet sinister ***Doctor Death***

There are many, many more possibilities contained within the generator, but this gives a quick idea of what you can get out of it. Feel free to mix and match words from different columns in an order other than specified; the exercise in lateral thinking will assist in developing the skills needed to solve bigger problems later on as the Brutality Crusade gets rolling full steam ahead. Remember, **you are a vigilante**, a superhero, one who steps above, around and beyond the strictures which bind normal mortals into a stagnant reality which crushes their dreams. The more skill developed in tweaking the parameters of an issue, the more successful you'll end up being.

{CHAPTER 4} DRESS FOR SUCCESS: MASKS, SPANDEX, BODY ARMOUR AND UTILITY BELTS

This guy has the right idea!

You've likely heard that old saying "Dress for the job you want", but probably never bothered thinking about why it's a saying in the first place. The reason is that for every endeavor there is a right way and a wrong way to prepare for what it brings...imagine a firefighter in a 3-piece suit; classy, but not very flame resistant. Or how about a Fortune 500 executive wearing booty shorts and a halter top? Not too likely he'll close the deal with the Japanese. Likewise, a shooter girl in a strip club won't get any tips if she's wearing a full Nomex bodysuit; that probably would work better for the firefighter though.

13

The point is that every vocation has come to be associated with certain clothing and equipment, and ignoring it can lead to disastrous results. It's not always merely a matter of fashion, either, as the poor soon to be crispy firefighter from the above example makes abundantly clear. The same goes for becoming a danger loving, rule breaking violent vigilante; although you won't have to worry about the boss refusing to grant that juicy promotion, you'll find that the consequences of ignoring finding the proper gear will be immensely detrimental...death **is** detrimental, right? Okay then, now that everyone's got with the program, let's get started.

Masks:

Ah yes, masks, one of the most iconic pieces of the heroic wardrobe. One can barely say the word superhero without a mask popping into the mind's eye, and for good reason. They add an air of mystery and anonymity; psychological research into the issue has shown that people report feeling far more anonymous while wearing a mask. It's like the freedom one gets as part of a mob, without the need for an unwieldy, attention grabbing crowd. Need to trigger the mental transformation from everyday consciousness into the ready for rage, come-hell-or-high-water, bullets don't stop me action time? Well shit, just pull your signature mask into place, and feel the craziness flow. So yeah, I guess masks are a no-brainer, right?

Wrong.
Masks are great for the above-mentioned reasons, and will make it harder to identify you if spotted by witnesses whilst pummeling a deserving sleaze-bucket, but certain considerations must be made. For one thing, unless it's winter, you'll look pretty fucking weird roaming around town with a mask on at all times...sorry, but this ain't a comic book, and the police *will* come to investigate the reports of the whackadoo dressed like a ninja/terrorist/etc. This means that if on foot you'll need a mask which fits easily into a pocket, which precludes the hard variety; this means cloth, unless you want to have a hard mask shoved in a backpack.

Now, I'm not saying that masks are a bad idea, in fact, quite the opposite. There is just the need to look closer at what is offered, and how to narrow the options down to fit your unique hero needs. With that in mind, let the mask parade begin!

Hard masks: These can actually provide varying levels of protection in addition to maintaining anonymity; the level of protection depends a lot on what you're willing to spend, as well as how important aesthetics are. Paintball masks come in the widest variety of designs, so much so that virtually anyone will find a style to match their imaginings, no matter how picky. They are aimed at stopping little gelatin balls filled with paint, though, and will therefore do almost nothing to mitigate the effects of getting fists, feet or baseball bats in the face.

Ballistic face masks are a whole different matter though. These lovely Justice accessories can easily be bought in protection levels up to 3A, meaning you don't have to worry about pretty much any common handgun caliber bullet ruining your day. As they are backed with impact reducing foam in key areas, your precious face will remain looking mostly the same as before getting shot, and punches will certainly hurt them more than they hurt you. Combine one of these babies with a ballistic helmet, and let the bullets fly! The main downside: a $350 price-tag...eek!

Soft masks: So very much variety to choose from! If you choose to go with a soft mask, wow, narrowing it down will take a while. There's the good old-fashioned camouflage mask, naturally, which can be digi-cam, traditional, "real tree", urban camo...did I mention there's lots of choice? Sticking with the camouflage for now, there's also mesh versus solid cloth, one-hole balaclava style, or versions with a mouth hole. **Note:** masks with the mouth hole are better at not fogging up glasses or sunglasses; some solid cloth masks have mesh over the mouth hole to hide the mouth while preventing fogging up of glasses.

Nomex and Kevlar masks are available in balaclava or mouth-hole varieties as well; Nomex provides flame resistance, while Kevlar is good for slash protection. Are you going to be getting burnt or slashed at more often? These are the sorts of things which need to be examined, and why there's no one answer which fits all hero types.

Biker culture has made it so a wide variety of aesthetic balaclava style masks exist to be worn under motorcycle helmets. For those desiring a Grim Reaper type of image, to put the fear of God into all who transgress, skull face designs are easy to find. Websites devoted to the love of all which surrounds the military are good places to look for such things as well. Custom masks are also available from vendors catering to the cosplay community, if you need a truly one-of-a-kind look; no matter how bizarre a design, they've seen weirder, trust me.

Which is better, soft or hard? This will depend on your usual method of operation; someone on foot patrol a bunch will be well served by a soft mask in a pocket, to be donned at the appropriate time. Someone patrolling on a motorcycle could wear a soft mask under the helmet, or pair it with a ballistic face mask (some are designed to work with helmets). The SWAT-styled superhero that kicks his way into action, busting down doors should probably have a ballistic mask for sure. The hero who patrols in a car or other vehicle can choose either type, leaving it off until it's time to save the day.

Spandex:

Ah spandex, the mainstay of comic book heroes and heroines throughout the ages. Who can deny the visual spectacle of chiseled pecs and rock hard abs, or heaving breasts straining to burst through their fabric prison? It has become so iconic that any real life hero planning on employing this wonder fabric must certainly put in countless hours at the gym and count every calorie, right?

Nope!
The beautiful people are certainly free to clad themselves in skin-tight glory, but the true, crime-fighting benefit is given to those who have zero right to wear it in normal society. The more outrageously lumpy and astoundingly ugly, the better, in fact. **Whale Man** should

consider spandex far more seriously than **Muscle Girl, Beautiful Destroyer of Miscreants.** Let me explain, because you're probably scratching your head in confusion at this point. Consider the following scenario:

It's a busy night in downtown Toronto, the sort of night where anything seems possible. Single folks can meet their soul-mates in lavish clubs; high-power businessmen conclude shady deals in upscale strip clubs; street performers can make more per hour than recent university graduates...and unwary revelers can end up beaten, mugged and raped in the back alleys between the well-lit main arteries of the urban jungle.

One of those unwary souls is about to find this out the hard way; happily, drunkenly making his way down a half-lit alley, the potential victim doesn't notice two men emerge from their predatory waiting post between a couple of dumpsters. Before his rum-soaked brain can even register what gives, they have bracketed him front and back, cutting off all hope of escape.

"Hand over all your stuff, and maybe we won't stab you too much!" declares one of the scruffy thugs. Shaking like a leaf, the poor fellow reaches into his pockets, hoping, praying that he might make it out alive...and then a "thud!" is heard.

A tall, obese figure rises from his crouch, knees straightening after absorbing the force from his fast-rope descent to the alley beneath his stealthy stake-out position far above. The would-be muggers turn to face this new threat, and get a bemused look upon their unshaven faces, as the tall, fat man has a brightly coloured mask on, which seems to clash with the dark trench coat he is wearing. Just as they start to come up with something to say, however, he rips the coat off, flinging it forcefully to the ground, revealing a skin-tight, multi-colour spandex suit, barely containing the rolls of flab all over his lumpy body.

*"I am the **Toxic Whale, Brutal Raper of Criminals!**" he declares in a booming voice, as he begins to sprint straight at them. They get a look of shock on their faces, hypnotized by the undulating motion of*

so much flesh jiggling all over the place. Shock turns to abject terror as they spot his utility belt, festooned with a wide variety of dildos, all of them rather large as well. The heroic figure pulls a gigantic black double-ended dildo from his belt with a flourish, and starts swinging it in a dazzling display of nunchaku style skill, reminiscent of Bruce Lee...if Bruce Lee were 6'6" and weighed 360 pounds, that is. This is too much for the fearful criminals, and they run away, hurtling down the alley and onto the street, screaming in a high pitch wail of cowardice.

His work done, the towering hero of a man climbs the fire escape back to the rooftops, there to resume his vigil. The drunken man who had come so close to harm just stands there, frozen in place for a couple of minutes with his hand still on the wallet. He then shakes his head, puts the wallet safely away, and vows to never tell anyone of what just occurred; no one would ever believe him anyway.

Police artist's rendition, based on fragmented reports.

See what I mean? If he had been clad in body armour, or leather protective gear, it would not have accentuated his greatest strength for crime-fighting, which is sheer shock value. Leather or armour would have held everything in place, more or less, negating the visual impact unique to that body type. Sure he could still have prevailed, but it might have involved a fight; with the awesome power of spandex and flab, however, the criminals lost their nerve immediately. Even if they had held their ground, they'd be at great disadvantage, because, by thinking through his unique hero style and body type, the **Toxic Whale** managed to create a powerfully disturbing image, one which saps the enemy of resolve, and makes them feel like a victim rather than a combatant.

If you want this awesome power for yourself, and share the same physical attributes, then spandex might be the right choice for you.

<u>Body Armour</u>:

Can't decide which armour to wear for today's mission? Let your cats help you make the correct choice!

Quick question: do you like getting shot? How about stabbed? Perhaps getting beaten with sticks till your organs bleed makes you happy...if you answered "Yes!" to any of those questions, then forget about body armour. It won't make you happy, and will only get in the way of having a good time.

For everyone else though, body armour merits serious consideration. Let's face it; people are going to get annoyed at you during the course of being a violent, crime-fighting vigilante. Hell, people even try shooting or stabbing the cops, and they have numbers on their side (being the biggest gang around, generally), in addition to societally sanctioned authority backed up by the full force of law. If people will attack them, you better believe they'll do it to you, given half a chance. Plus, it just looks damn cool, so if your modus operandi won't be affected by body armour, go for it! And for people who can't have an overt type, we'll examine some low-key options that might just be what the Justice Doctor ordered.

Chainmail: A classic choice which has survived the test of time, chainmail offers great slash protection, and okay stab protection. Modern variants are based on the electronically welded stainless steel ring design of those shark suits divers wear; if it'll stop a Great White, it should do pretty good against knives, generally. As many dead people could tell you though—if they weren't dead, that is—it does fuck all against bullets, and arrows tend to get through it as well. **Benefit:** the concealed, modern type works well under normal clothing or even spandex, as it's soft/cloth-like in nature; it conforms to the shape of the body. The overt type can be worn around town too, and cops generally don't care as it won't stop bullets...you may be looked at like some sort of mega-dork, though. **Cons:** It won't stop bullets!

Polycarbonate Anti-Stab Vest: Cheaper than bullet resistant vests, this type of armour is marketed to security guards, corrections officers, and cops in areas which are more stabby than gun-happy. Available in both 0.125 and 0.250 inch thicknesses, it works great against slashes, and will even stop two-handed sword thrusts, axe hits, and tomahawk spike attacks. Some have additional foam padding which will make you practically invulnerable to blunt attacks, including baseball bat strikes. With both overt and covert options available, you can go for anything from the bulked up badass look, to having it hidden under a t-shirt. They even have an option which looks like a suit vest, so you can get fancy with that shit and wear it to the opera! **Cons:** At close range it will print (be visible) under a t-shirt, at least a tad. It also won't stop bullets.

Kevlar or Spectra Vest: This is the classic "Bullet Proof Vest" (actually, they're bullet resistant, not fully bullet proof). The layers of dense, tightly woven aramid fibers catch the projectile, deforming it and preventing penetration. Available in overt and covert options, you can advertise your armoured might to the world at large, or go incognito. The classic "bullet proof vest" won't do shit to stop knives or arrows though...purely ballistic protection. **Cons:** You can still get shanked by some skinny-assed crack-head.

Kevlar or Spectra with Wire/Chainmail Variant: In order to address the getting stabbed by skinny crack-head issue, manufacturers have made vests which add a layer of chainmail or wire mesh, in order to provide stab resistance. **Cons:** it's gonna be bulky; unless you're wearing a winter coat, folks will see it.

Plate Carriers, Ceramic/Metal/Kevlar/Spectra Plates and Dragon Skin...Oh My: If you need to jump in the path of high-powered rifle rounds, you need this option. It offers the best protection level, along with customization potential up the wazoo. A plate carrier is basically a vest with pockets to put bullet or stab resistant plates in. Sometimes the carrier itself is made of Kevlar, but generally isn't. Depending on what level of threat you'll be facing, you choose Kevlar or Spectra plates, or ceramic plates, and possibly throw in a titanium or stainless steel plate for stab protection. Titanium or steel plates capable of stopping rifle rounds on their own are available as well, but weigh a fair bit. The great thing about this option is that you can start cheap, and build up multi-mission capability as you go along (and get more cash); the customization level is cool too. You can add rubber shock-absorbing trauma plates as well, to absorb impact...bullets, knives, bats, punches...you're pretty much fucking invulnerable if you choose the correct mix.

Dragon Skin armour is just a more flexible option, based on the same technology but more manufacturing and cost intensive. It consists of a whole bunch of tiny, overlapping ceramic plates held in a Kevlar vest. You'll have more maneuverability, but far less cash...better have a few thousand or more dollars to invest if you want it. **Cons:** All these options, including Dragon Skin, are pretty darn bulky; you just can't get the ability to take multiple rifle round impacts in a slim package...that just ain't gonna happen.

Riot and Cell Extraction Armour: Get armoured head to toe and go out there and brawl! This option is aimed at dealing with folks who are really, really pissed off but don't have any guns. It offers pretty much the best all-around impact protection, and for an additional fee you can get it with slash/stab resistance. Helmet, shoulder guards, vambraces, gauntlets, thigh and shin protection, vests...you can get it all. **Cons:** Super bulky, and won't stop bullets.

Miscellaneous: If you shop around, it is possible to find stab/slash and/or bullet resistant products to cover most of your body; neck; shoulders; elbows; forearms; thighs; shins...bring enough cash for the ride, and something truly terrifying can emerge on the other side. **Cons:** There will still be weak spots a lucky shot could get through, and good luck running with that extra 100 pounds of stuff on you.

Bullet Proof clothing: Thanks to the modern age of violence and paranoia, there does exist an option that will work for almost any hero, even if they want to remain low key. I saved what may be the best for last...Bullet-resistant suit jackets and other coats.

That's right; you can go dressed to the nines and still be ready for action! Want to look like a respectable businessman until you mask-up and punch evil into submission? Just search the web for level 3A ballistic protection in a stylish 3-piece suit! Or perhaps you want to look cool and relaxed while lurking in that alley...how about a Kevlar lined denim or leather jacket? Wear it over-top of a slash resistant, Kevlar lined shirt (long or short sleeve), and now you can handle most threats you're likely to face while out for a hot night of vengeance.

Gloves:

Okay, so you're armoured and masked-up, prepared to grapple the miscreants prior to pummeling them into submission...you'll probably be using hands, right? You aren't going to be using bare hands I hope; I mean, come on, who knows what diseases they have! At least two-thirds of regular folks don't bother to wash their hands, and that's before you add a major methamphetamine addiction into the mix. That addict you're wrestling probably sucked a goodly number of cocks before deciding to rob a gas station. Toilet seats in public restrooms are likely cleaner than the vast majority of street-level thugs requiring a sound thrashing, so unless you really want Hepatitis C, HIV, Herpes, Staphylococcus, and some germ new to science (discovered for the first time in you as you slowly waste away), put on a pair of gloves.

But as with most things, gloves aren't a one-size-fits-all proposition either. By looking at the various benefits offered by all the different options, though, you'll easily arrive at a decision which perfectly fits your busy vigilante lifestyle.

Cut-Resistant Gloves: These generally use either a Kevlar or Spectra lining, occasionally with glass fibers added into the proprietary blend. As competition for cash is fierce, companies continually research new materials to satisfy the needs of industrial and crime-fighting end users. Most superheroes will likely go with a classic black leather glove for the outer shell, which does blend in well with casual wear, while still looking good as an accessory to more exotic gear. But fear not if your tastes are more colourful; a wide range of colours and fabrics are available, enough to match any outfit. Kevlar gloves with no outer shell are readily available as well at all industrial safety supply stores, and can be worn under any glove of your choice.

Hard-Knuckle Gloves: A great choice for bashing teeth out of a deserving scum's mouth. ☺ These gloves have hard material molded into a knuckle guard which then protects the knuckles (obviously). You'll want to try them on in person, as not all are created equal; some which are aimed at knuckle protection for extrication operations or motorcycle riding work well for a back-hand hit, but not when doing regular punches. Gloves aimed at riot control and military usage tend to be pretty good, but it's still best to try them out first. If one shops around enough, it is possible to find gloves with hard knuckles and cut-resistance all in one. Carbon fiber, titanium, Kevlar, and high-impact plastics have all been used as protective material. Check out the local motorcycle shop for all your crazy colour needs, although the palm padding sometimes impedes weapon usage.

Sap Gloves: Generally made of leather, they are constructed with a pouch containing steel or lead shot/powder. Although it adds a little mass for a blow, the main thing is how they cushion the knuckles upon impact while still transferring the force. As one notable superhero says, "They impart the impact while protecting and padding my knuckles. I could punch evil all day!" 'Nuff said. Also available with Kevlar lining for slash resistance; I heartily recommend them.

Gauntlets: This refers to gloves where the protection comes up along the forearm, sometimes right up to the elbow. Military, riot control/ cell extractions, as well as motorcycle riding varieties are all available, some with Kevlar or Spectra lining. If you patrol on a motorcycle, the motorcycle ones will blend right in. Military variations will be best for firing weapons and manipulating knives, whereas the riot control ones will be best for the "Hulk Smash!" style of heroics.

If you want variety, you're in luck! There are styles with hard knuckles, padded knuckles, and even padded forearms with plastic or titanium trauma plates for blocking bats, sticks, and other assorted impact threats. Get online and give your credit card a workout.

Footwear:

Now that your hands are protected, it's time to get the feet covered as well. Feet are a fairly integral part of crime-fighting; unless you're a paraplegic sniper or cyber vigilante, there's going to be plenty of walking, kicking, stomping and leaping. At first, the temptation will be to just go with whatever looks cool...fight that urge! A trend following party girl may end up with cramped feet and have to take a cab home; a superhero with bleeding feet and a raw Achilles tendon may end up stabbed, shot or incarcerated. In order to avoid such pitfalls, gain the necessary information ahead of time.

Steel-toed Boots: For many hero types, a sturdy pair of leather boots with steel toes and a steel plate in the bottom is just the ticket. Conversely, one can go with a composite material toe cap and shank, which will be just as protective but with less weight. Whichever way one goes, however, make sure the pair you choose gets broken in nicely before using them on patrols; those annoying blisters could steal attention away from more important things at a critical moment! The choice between the two options is entirely personal preference, but I suggest trying both out. For kicking down doors, some may prefer the solid heft of the steel version, although the ankle support is probably more important in reality, as far as transfer of energy is concerned.

Heroes who find themselves running frequently will probably find the lighter weight of the composite material to be of benefit, and good ankle support might just be the difference between evading capture by the cops, and getting hard prison time because of a busted ankle when landing from a jump. Whether kicking down doors, running towards crime or evading pursuit, most heroes report that an 8 to 10-inch height is best in a boot. All the colours of the rainbow are available, so accessorizing to your overall look is easy.

Running Shoes/Boots: Perhaps you have no intention of ever kicking down a door, and stomping through dirty alleys ain't your thing. Perhaps you want to leap from and between tall buildings, in seeming defiance of gravity...at heart you are a Parkour/Free-running machine. You need something made of space age materials, assembled with toxic adhesives brewed deep in the laboratories of mad scientists...

Lucky for you, there's big money in this type of item, so the selection is gigantic. Every main brand like Nike, Adidas, and all the rest have shoes aimed right at this form of craziness, plus a bunch of others that will work out too. Extra cushion soles; super lightweight materials...

you can even add puncture resistant insoles and Kevlar laces that won't rip practically ever. Zany colours or subdued tones, high-top boots or low cut shoes, the choices are almost endless. Don't be surprised if you end up with so many pairs that the question to one's spouse becomes "Honey, which pair goes best with my titanium frame .357 Magnum revolver?"

Utility Belt or Cargo Pants...The Battle Continues:

Right, you're kitted out head to toe, with a stylish mask that accentuates your body armour, gloves perfect for punching evil all day, and a pair of boots fit for a god. Now you'll just put your extendable baton and snazzy semi-auto pistol...where, exactly? Hey, what about the handcuffs and the night vision monocular; fuck, there's no room for any of that shit in this getup!

Yep, you've run up against that old dilemma; **where do I put my stuff?** For most folks that's why they buy a house in the first place, to have somewhere to put all their stuff. You have the added hassle of figuring out how to carry a bunch of stuff, and have it easily accessible; a tall order, to be sure. But don't fret, easy answers are at hand. It's simply a matter of figuring out whether a utility belt or cargo pants will fit your unique personal style best.

Utility belt: When you think utility belt in a superhero context, what pops to mind? Answer: Batman, of course. But you know what pops to mind when normal folks see someone wearing one who isn't a cop or security personnel of some kind? Answer: "Hey look at that fucking dork who thinks he's Batman or something! Ha ha ha, what a goddamned loser!" Point being, you're gonna stand out, and not in a good way.

The only way this works for the purposes of vigilantes is if:

1) You're driving around in your car, and only jump out to fight crime when you see it. All people see normally is your head, so they don't notice anything out of place.

2) Part of your walking around garb includes a trench coat or other such garment which covers it up.

3) You're kicking a door down and raiding a drug house, kitted up like SWAT with overt body armour, and possibly a bullet-resistant mask. In this case, a utility belt just adds to the overall effect.

4) The chosen disguise for walking around involves hiding in plain sight as a security guard; once again, the utility belt just completes the look. You'll fade into the background, dismissed as an irrelevant nobody.

That's pretty much it. For everything else, **cargo pants are the way to go.** Plenty of storage for all your various gear items, and with an inside the waistband holster you can conceal guns, knives, batons, and other such goodies. Oh yeah, and for the above-mentioned times when a duty belt doesn't compromise mission success, cargo pants go along with utility belts to complete the look (which is good, because then you can devote the extra storage space in the pants to handy items like bombs and various other goodies ☺).

Whew, that sure was a bunch of stuff to consider, but now you're ready to take to the streets in style. With some brutal honesty on your part, an outfit which inspires fear/preserves anonymity/offers great protection (or whatever else is needed...hey, time to hero-up and figure some of that shit out for yourself!) will emerge. A unique style of vigilante is being carefully crafted, soon to embark upon a Justice Rampage of epic proportion. Well, once you've got a few more things, that is; it's time to get physical!

{CHAPTER 5} WHOA, I KNOW KUNG FU...
LEARNING THE FINE ART OF KICKING ASS

Okay, I know you're all gung-ho to run out and clean the mean streets of scum. You feel ready, you feel powerful, and those poses in the mirror look really sweet with all the armour and whatnot. I get it...it's completely natural.

It's also premature.
Don't believe me? That's cool, but check this little scenario out before making any fatally rash decisions:

A powerfully built figure stalks through the night, exuding confidence and menace in equal measure. The citizens he passes by instinctively avert their eyes, without quite knowing why; is it the look of grim determination is his eyes, his purposeful stride, or might it be the air of mystery a smartly cut black trench coat creates? Whatever it is, this dude has it in spades, and woe to any street-rat that crosses his path.

Having turned down a less traveled side street, he witnesses a crime in progress! Three urban youths, probably between the ages of 18 and 21, have decided to do a smash and grab on a convenience store closed for the night (not very convenient for paying customers, being closed, but very convenient for criminal scum). One of them has just hurled a cinderblock through the main display window, and another one clears the jagged glass out of the way with a baseball bat; clearly, this is not the first time they've committed such an act. The third man of the evil trio keeps a wary eye out for cops, or possibly any other thugs looking to jump their criminal claim.

"Yes!" the watchful hero declares, "This is a perfect use of my skills; these dorks stand not a chance!" With intentions declared to God Almighty Himself, he pulls on his stylish—yet threatening—mask, and does a quick gear check; sap gloves are in place, anti-stab vest

is tightly fastened, and his 21 inch ASP extendable baton is ready to go. It's show-time!

The scum on lookout detail notices something is up...there appears to be a masked man wearing armour charging towards their position, with trench coat flapping to dramatic effect. "Yo, Zack, Chris, get over here! Some freak is fixing to mess our shit up! I need back-up, now!" Temporarily abandoning their larceny, the other two join their partner in crime, and quickly reach a unanimous decision; it's time to beat the living shit out of this costumed freak.

The stage is now set, and battle is joined; the towering, heroic figure snaps his baton into attack configuration, and leaps into the fray, heedless of danger. This doesn't faze his opponents, however, for they have been fighting on the mean streets since they were old enough to skip school. Thus, the first strike of the would-be hero misses the mark, and he is placed off balance momentarily...and a moment is all they need. A baseball bat into his upper arm breaks bone, and the ASP falls to the ground with a sad clank. This is followed by a punch to the head from the side, which knocks him to the ground; then the stomping fun begins!

*The three thugs all commence to kick him all over, laughing and jumping on him too; "Hey watch me, I'm Bruce Lee!" says one as he lands a double foot stomp following a jump. As consciousness fades and he prays for a slight chance at survival, one final thought flows through the hero-turned-victim's head; **"I probably should have learned how to fight first."***

Wow, that's a heaping helping of sober-the-fuck-up right there. I'll bet you were reading along, picturing the triumphant conclusion to our hero's charge to glory as if it were you. Probably wanted to stop picturing yourself in his place towards the end though, am I right? Well, if you don't want to end your brutal career in such a painful, pathetic way, fear not, for we're going to discover the skills you need. ☺ So grab a coffee, settle in and join me as we explore the wonderful world of **martial arts**, and separate the really effective from the marketing bullshit.

Get the fuck off the couch and practice!

Krav Maga: Often touted as the perfect martial art for those wanting realistic combat skills, it has been battle tested in the Middle East by Israeli soldiers under conditions where failure equals death. A slightly modified form has been taught to civilians for quite some time as well. Krav Maga would seem to embody the term **martial art** quite well, being as the terminology is supposed to mean military art.

So go out and sign up for classes right now, correct? Not so quick, young Grasshopper, there is more to the story that you need to know. For although Krav Maga does indeed contain many simple, direct ways of dealing with weapons threats, as well as strategies to combat multiple assailants, the hard-core training groups are few and far between. You see, we live in a world of weaklings (which is why you need to rise to fight evil, remember?), and this has led to most schools becoming glorified dance classes.

If you can find an actual, bona fide Krav Maga group which doesn't mind the occasional serious injury during training, then sure, go for it. It will get you up to speed fairly quickly as opposed to some arts, while still allowing for life-long progression in ass-kicking skills. Given the unique demands of your chosen path, however, there may be better choices...keep reading.

Taekwondo: The hero just starting out may be tempted to take Taekwondo, if only because it is the single most prevalent martial art in North America, Korea, etc. Its inclusion as an official Olympic sporting event has spread it far and wide. In many small towns, it may be the **only** martial art there...and that's probably the only time you should take it.

"What?" I hear you ask. "If it's good enough to be an Olympic sport, why not take it?"
Because it's an Olympic sport, that's why.
Not only was it sporting enough in general practice to get included, now most places sport it up even more, ignoring the most vital aspects for actual fighting. There's not enough emphasis on hand and other upper body techniques, generally only about 30 percent, tops. Even the scoring system only reinforces this; two points for a kick to the head, one point for a punch to the body, with **no head punches allowed at all.**

That's right, you practice head punches, but not by punching each other in the head. You practice blocks against punches to the head, but you never have to block punches intentionally aimed at your head with intent to strike! The ones in practice are done in as contrived a fashion as most schools do knife defense practice, with the attack known ahead of time, often performed slowed down, and only one at a time. ITF—International Taekwondo Federation—at least allows back-fists to the side and top of the head during sparring, but still no straight punches to the head (or hooks, uppercuts, overhand rights, chops, etc.). WTF—World Taekwondo Federation—is the one sanctioned by the Olympics, and it allows no hand strikes to the head in sparring, period. This has led to many schools adopting a guard with hands down very low, making it very easy to punch them in the head; they can do this because a kick moves slower than a punch, and has to come further to reach head level, giving time to block still.

So, if you want to develop fighting skills that facilitate getting punched in the head, take Taekwondo, especially the WTF sanctioned style. You can also learn how to get kicked in the balls, foot-swept, and kicked in the legs, as no attacks below the belt are allowed in sparring, and rarely if ever practiced.

The only reason to take this is if no other, more practical styles are available in your area, as it does at least practice punching, kicking and blocking; you will at least get used to attacks coming at you and not flinching. Can also be used as a supplemental art to get plenty of practice with head height and jumping/spinning kicks...it has plenty of those.

Kung Fu/Gung Fu/Wushu: Originating as Chinese traditional martial arts, Kung Fu and related terms encompass a wide range of styles with a wide range of philosophies. They differentiate into "hard" and "soft" ("external" and "internal") styles; some supposedly mimic the movements and attack strategies of animals; some claim to be awesome battle powers developed by mystical monks...it doesn't matter. The important thing is to go check out the individual school in your area, if there is one.

You see, some styles are just glorified interpretive dance; others are meditation for health purposes; some are great ways of kicking ass. If you're lucky, you'll find a school which uses takedowns, throws, groundwork and low strikes in their sparring, along with punching/ elbowing the head. These styles aimed at modern competition and defense incorporate the lessons MMA (mixed martial arts) made clear, blending them with the best that tradition preserved from the past. These places could provide what you need, or at least part of it.

Karate: Originating in Japan, Karate now acts as an umbrella term for a multitude of stylistic variations. Everything from Kempo, to Shorin-ryu, Shotokan, Kyokushin, and a whole whack-load more. Some are basically Taekwondo taught by a different name with alternate patterns—a pre-arranged series of moves used to develop technique and flow in movement—whereas others are fucking hard-core.

Kyokushin, for instance, is noted for its full-contact sparring and emphasis on conditioning the body. Founded by Masutatsu Oyama, who was a legendary badass himself; he fought something like 52 bulls, killing 3 with his bare hands; he chopped the horns off most of the rest. This level of awesomeness earned him the name of **Godhand**, which isn't a bad superhero name either, come to think of it. ☺

As with Kung Fu, check out the various schools to determine the level of vigilante preparation suitability; many schools are adding grappling while standing and on the ground in order to get in on the MMA competitions, which is where the action is tending to be more and more.

Mixed Martial Arts: The coming of MMA has changed the contemporary martial arts scene. More a philosophy than a specific style, the idea at its most basic is that one must be able to fight standing up as well as on the ground. In addition, if you want to fight standing up, you must be able to keep from being taken to the ground. It became popularized in the 1990's by the Ultimate Fighting Championship (which started in 1993), and was a slap in the face to many "traditional martial artists", who all thought their style ruled all. One martial art that did well was Brazilian Jiu-Jitsu, because they had already mixed fighting standing with fighting on the ground.

It is not really a new concept though; generations of smart fighters/ martial artists did it all the time! Bruce Lee cross-trained with people from different arts; people would take boxing and mix it with Judo; Taekwondo mixed with wrestling, etc. The new thing is simply the rise of training camps and schools devoted to it, making it simpler to do it all at once, which is a good thing...and it usually beats watching boxing on pay-per-view.

Judo: Developed by Jigoro Kano, it takes Japanese Jujutsu and changes things so that it can be practiced full force with less injuries. Throws where you don't break the elbow, moves aimed at getting a submission rather than tearing tendons off, etc. The benefit is that it provides great ground movement skills and some good chokes, and can be practiced against full resistance. On its own, not so great, but mixes very well with striking arts.

Boxing: You're gonna learn how to punch! You'll also learn how to take a punch, as well as how to duck, dodge, block or roll with them. With great emphasis on getting in shape and overall body conditioning, boxing mixes well with grappling arts, and will even add to other striking arts. Add the benefits of the "Sweet Science" to your bag of deadly tricks.

Kickboxing: Basically, it adds kicking to boxing (duh!). Well, there are actually some pretty big differences between all of what goes as kickboxing. Some allow elbows, foot sweeps, clinches, etcetera, whereas others limit the use of those. Many MMA gyms will have a kickboxing instructor as part of the team; in general, it can be a decent part of an overall combative strategy. Mix with a grappling option of your choice and see what results!

Aikido: Noted for its many locks, throws, and flowing footwork, this Japanese art can make a great addition to the street-level hero's skillset. Not so great on its own though, as mastering the system takes many, many years, and employs no strikes except as distraction. It will give greater insight into using an opponent's energy against them, though.

Hapkido: An eclectic Korean martial art, Hapkido combines the stand-up grappling, throws and locks from Aikido with the strikes of Taekwondo. With a greater emphasis on hand and other upper body strikes, it will give battle readiness more quickly. Many schools are also including ground-fighting and lower body strikes now, making this a great choice to put the hurt on crime.

Filipino Martial arts: Comprised of individual styles such as Arnis, Eskrima and Kali, these dudes are noted for their skill with weapons, mostly blades and sticks. There is also great emphasis on being able to transition fluidly from armed to empty hand combat, and a realization of the underlying similarities in body mechanics behind both. The skill developed tends to help when fighting unarmed against people with weapons; something to keep in mind.

Combatives: This broad category is made up of systems based on combat techniques taught during previous wars (World War Two combatives are quite popular), and systems taught to current military or police/security forces around the world. There are truly the absolute best skills *and* the very worst crap to be found amongst those offering training in this. You'll either be training with truly serious students completely dedicated to being the best, or a bunch of old fat guys who have a severe allergy to cardiovascular exercise. Research the hell out of anyone offering this stuff, and even then, good luck; it's truly a minefield of gigantic egos, outright lies, and bullshit artists.

While there are a butt-load of other martial arts styles out there, this list gives you a pretty good overview, at least enough to decide where to go from here. Remember to keep calm, do the research, and don't believe anyone's credentials just because of all the shiny trophies and certificates with Japanese writing on them.

Also, your unique needs to be fulfilled by this will be different than the average person. You might need to get good at dealing with knife attacks and beating people to death with a steel rod; Filipino Martial Arts could get you where you need to be in a hurry! Or how about the fact that MMA practice still outlaws biting, fish-hooking, shots to the groin, small joint manipulation, eye gouging, and an ever increasing list of "dirty moves"? A crime-fighting superhero needs to be ready for all those attacks, and might even want to use them himself! That's something to think long and hard on, before settling into a training routine. Never forget where all this is headed.

Okay, so you have a name; suitable apparel for battling evildoers; your unique hero type; and now may even have an idea of which martial art will help get the requisite combat skills. That's a bunch of stuff to figure out...maybe it's time to chill for a bit; let's go for a nice relaxing car ride!

{CHAPTER 6} CARS, TRUCKS, BUSSES, TRAINS AND MOTORCYCLES...OR A SKATEBOARD? HEROES IN MOTION

Planes, trains and automobiles; us humans sure like moving around from place to place. Whether we actually need to get there or are just bored by the colour of the wallpaper at home, there's an almost incessant need to feel like we're doing *something*. It's simply a basic human trait...and it's one shared by criminals as well, which is why you need to figure out a way to get around for the imposition of harsh Justice.

But it's not just about getting there, is it? There's also the small matter of getting away after; avoiding unwanted attention; weapons storage; how the vehicle affects deployment speed to bash the scum when located, and possibly looking cool in the process. Many of those concerns aren't something the normal person buying a used car needs to think about, but heroes generally do. Just look at this list of things you need to consider:

- Is there enough trunk space for a human body or two?
- Does this vehicle have crash avoidance features which make it impossible to run people over? How can it be disabled so I can run people over, if need be?
- Can it be shut down remotely by the cops, bringing an exciting, high speed getaway to a sad ending?
- How are the off-road capabilities? Can it at least jump a curb?
- If I have to ditch it in a lake somewhere, how much would a replacement cost?
- Is it a common enough vehicle to blend in with the rest of the traffic, enabling stealth operations?

By the way, that's just the beginning...you'll likely have a bunch of unique requirements as well once the mission planning begins. So, with all this in mind, let's begin exploring the options available to help give the capacity to reach out and crush someone.

Cars: They are pretty much the most common vehicles on the road, which is good for the purposes of blending in. Even a mid-size car will have enough trunk space to shove one or two people in, which can be good for getting them transported to your interrogation dungeon. Unless your weapon storage needs are massive, they should easily hold all the nifty crime-fighting devices required for all but the biggest operations. Most cars have a severe lack of off-road capability though, so if the need to speed across fields will ever come into play, another selection might be required. Try to look for slightly older models, without crash avoidance features, or any other "safety improvements" that could hamper a good Justice rampage. Used cars are cheaper to replace if need be anyway.

Pick-up Trucks and SUV's: These snazzy mechanical conveyances run the gamut from hard-core industrial and military workhorses to primped up Mid-life Crisismobiles. One thing to keep in mind right away is to check out wheelbase width to center of gravity ratio, as many have an unfortunate tendency to tip over when cornering at high speeds. Luckily, there are off-road racing magazines and websites that can get you up to speed on what exactly to look for, as well as ways to mitigate the issue.

As long as the tipping problem is avoided, they can make for a sturdy urban assault vehicle, able to ram vehicles for capturing crooks, or when escaping from misguided cops. Hopping curbs and running through the occasional field poses no issues for these behemoths, but they lag behind the humble car in standing out from the crowd. A big-ass truck or SUV stands out, which is why guys with small penises or huge fear of death just can't get enough of them. As a violent vigilante on a mission, though, this may not be what you want. Depending on where you live though, the truck/SUV population might be quite large, in which case it'll blend right in; so if you live such a city, or are doing missions out in the country where such vehicles actually serve a purpose, then by all means go for it!

They also have pretty good cargo capacity, and with a specialty truck topper or a cage separating the front of an SUV from the rear passenger compartment, can make a good snatch-and-grab mission vehicle; fill that dungeon in one or two trips. ☺

Vans: For the urban commando, nothing gives ultimate assault capacity quite like a cargo van. The varieties without much in the way of windows in the back section allow for carrying just about any crime-fighting, gang destroying weaponry you can imagine (and which I'll teach you to build in a later chapter). Whether you're changing into your fully armoured super-suit prior to charging into a heavily fortified drug house, or transporting a huge bomb with a radio controlled delivery system, a full-sized van will do the trick.

Motorcycles: Stylish, fast, and highly maneuverable, the motorcycle makes a great choice for certain mission types. For one thing, it allows one to wear full protection without looking like a freak; helmet, gloves, armoured jacket, all this and more can look entirely normal. Just motor on up to crime and crush it into oblivion! They work especially well when trying to target carjacking types; you see, when the carjacker (okay, bikejacker in this case) comes up to you, your mobility is unimpaired, so you can smash his head in with the handy hammer located in your saddlebag. This leads into weapon storage, a niche filled by saddlebags. Saddlebags give easy access to your tools of death, and riding a motorcycle allows for perfectly legal carry of certain items; hammers and heavy chains have legitimate uses in a motorcycle context.

You won't be carrying unconscious human bodies back to your dungeon with a motorcycle, but you'll certainly be able to create some corpses in style, and have a decent chance of evading capture, making a grand escape afterward. The ability to weave through traffic, ride along sidewalks, through alleys or even shopping malls will serve you well; definitely worth serious consideration.

Public Transport (Buses, Trolleys, Subways) and Taxis: Depending on your mission and the sort of city you live in, using the existing public transportation infrastructure may make good sense. Naturally, this will limit the quantity/type of weaponry which can be brought along, but not to such an extent as to get in the way of violent success. It also gives ready access to one type of crime not easily targeted when utilizing other modes of transportation; crime which targets and operates on public transit itself. The Guardian Angels started out mainly on the subways of New York...you may wish to try a similar crime-fighting venue. As long as your protective gear and weaponry is low-key, you'll blend right in; a hoody and an extendable baton might just be what the doctor ordered.

The cons are also readily apparent though, and may be enough to cause one to choose other options. For one thing, you must operate on their schedule, and many cities do not offer 24 hour per day service; what about when the urge to impose Justice upon an apathetic world strikes at 03:00 hours, eh? Getaways after vigilante Justice can be problematic as well; although movies show heroes jumping onto the back of moving streetcars, this doesn't happen in real life. The author can personally attest as to how aggravating it is when the bus pulls away despite the driver seeing you pounding on the door demanding entry, while an angry gang of armed criminals give chase from behind, swearing threats of imminent death; that was an interesting night.

Cabs are even more of a nuisance as they cost a bunch, and aren't always readily available, depending on how busy things are that night. One could, for an additional fee, have a cab standing by to give getaway transport, but then the driver might remember who that odd fare was that needed quick extraction from the vicinity where all those corpses were found the next day. Probably best to just avoid cabs entirely.

Bicycles and Skateboards: For stealthily sneaking up on drug dealers, muggers, and other street-level scum, nothing beats the humble bicycle or skateboard. They are also very, very cheap in comparison with other vehicular options, which makes them painless to dispose of, if need be. Throw them in a dumpster, a local crick, or just hurl them into a handy river. You can also find bicycles easily enough if on the run by foot; commandeer the first unchained bike in view and put some distance between you and your pursuers.

Skateboards can also be used as clubs for attack, or shields for defense; this is great for undercover Justice, where having dedicated weaponry on oneself might constitute a liability. Bikes can also be used to throw at assailants or parry a knife attack, but aren't nearly as good for makeshift weapons use. Both can often be taken on public transportation, although skateboards get the nod here; some buses and trolleys have bike racks on them, but not all, and subways generally don't allow bikes on board. Combining a bike or skateboard with public transit gives pretty good mobility in the urban jungle, certainly enough to make that option far more attractive.

Electric bikes are becoming more and more popular as time goes on, and have the same top speed (pretty much) as a bicycle, so I'll briefly discuss them. They too are rather silent, which makes them good for stealthy approach. They are heavier than a regular bike though, so not good for throwing or blocking knife/bat attacks in an emergency. Most importantly though, they are not cheap—at least not the decent ones—so aren't as great for ditching if need be. This is changing over time, however, so for some heroes they may fit their mobility requirements. Oh yeah, one last consideration is that you won't be able to take many models on public transit, so there is that; however, they can still be ridden at speed if one is injured during battle...it's for each individual to decide.

ATV's and Dirt Bikes: We often think of heroics as occurring in an urban setting, but evil is not contained by city limits! Rural transgressors must also get their comeuppance, and an All-Terrain Vehicle helps get the job done once one has left the beaten path behind. Dirt bikes fall under this category as well, for they are truly only 2-wheel variants; the basic rationale behind them remains the same.

Commonly available with 3, 4, 6 or 8 wheels, the ATV has become a staple of back-country recreation, hunting, and work. Due to the extremely high amount of people who manage to roll the 3-wheel variant, we'll discard it from the pool of crime-fighting options, as a broken neck won't get you closer to retribution. The four-wheel variety is available in a wide range of engine sizes and configurations, with some offering heavy duty gear carrying capacity (with a rack to mount stuff to on the back), while others aim at the high-flying stunt drivers. For the sort of raids one might choose a 4-wheeler for, something right in the middle of that range is likely best, as both speed and carrying some gear will help immensely.

For longer Justice Treks, the six or eight wheel versions with a cargo bed are best; the extra carrying capacity can be used for food, water, weaponry, perhaps a tent, and anything else which could contribute to mission success and battle readiness. They are also available in amphibious variants, which means they can travel through swampy areas and other bodies of water that would impede progress otherwise. Backwoods meth cookers will never be beyond your reach once one of these bad boys is added to the vehicular inventory.

Dirt bikes are great for off-road evil elimination when speed is of the essence; grab the handlebars, twist the throttle, and feel the wind whistle by. Just remember that a bigger engine gives more speed, but also adds weight; this can get it bogged down in mud, or make it harder to lift upright after wiping out...just something to keep in mind. One last thing in favour of dirt bikes is that with the addition of proper lights, signals and a license plate, it can be street legal, making for seamless transition from paved road ways to the backcountry wilds.

Boats: A great way to eliminate evil as it floats on the water, or hides upon some nondescript island. Crime isn't limited to the mainland, and you shouldn't be either. Suitable choices range from humble inflatable rafts and canoes, all the way up to luxury yachts, depending on budget and intended target. If one were wishing to stealthily approach a drug operation on a remote island in a remote, northern Canadian lake, an inflatable raft with a small docking motor to get within range, followed by rowing the final distance would be a grand choice...just remember those night vision goggles for navigating in the dark. On the other hand, if one is trying to lure

Caribbean pirates to attack his vessel in order to trap/execute them, a small luxury yacht would be far better suited to the task. The main thing to remember is don't get hung-up on a particular style of water craft just because it's cool, or fits the image you wish to portray; the mission is paramount, all else is of secondary concern.

Thus endeth the brief overview of vehicles suited for fighting crime, complete with brief observations as to suitability and points of concern. It is not exhaustive, as planes, trains and hovercraft are not touched upon; however, using a bit of your brainpower should allow you to figure when those options are suitable. One final vehicle not covered is the hover bike; as I write this, the hover bike is only about two years from availability to the public, and yes, it **is** as fucking cool as you might imagine. Two points work against it though; it will be priced about the same as a sports car, and it will attract massive attention. Attracting massive attention is something you really, really want to avoid as a vigilante superhero, as it will fuck up your mission objectives big time. Keep that in mind as we jet over to the next topic: Disguises.

{CHAPTER 7} DISGUISES: BECAUSE MASKS AREN'T ALWAYS AN OPTION

The mask has imprinted itself on our collective imaginations as the mainstay of disguising one's identity so thoroughly that few can imagine a superhero, vigilante, or even a bank robber without one. It is just so fucking iconic...I'll bet you had a mask design in mind before you even began reading this book, didn't you?

Well, it's time to get real here folks; masks are not always an option, and even when they are, may not be the most effective means of maintaining anonymity. As in other sections, I present an example for your consideration, one in which a mask would not have been anywhere near as effective as the methods employed:

The hero hears sirens approaching in the distance as he tries to slow his breathing after the exertion just ended. Three dead muggers lay at his feet, their blood already forming little pools. He looks around momentarily, deciding which way to go in order to make his escape; one path leads right to a main road, while another has a small group just forming, as people come to satisfy their curiosity and see what all the commotion was about. A third route, however, is clear and leads in a direction which works for the plan he has; route confirmed, the vigilante races down the alleyway on foot.

Not long after this, the police arrive at the crowd of onlookers, and get a good description of the perp; wide-brimmed hat; black jacket; leather gloves; dark cargo pants; long, blond hair; full, almost puffy cheeks; one person even noticed his piercing blue eyes. Unknown to the crowd or the police, however, this description is already incorrect by the time they're hearing it, for the hero had planned for such an eventuality. As he rounds the first corner leading off of the initial alley into another, the hat gets tossed into a handy dumpster, and the jacket now appears to be an attractive shade of blue rather than black...it's a reversible jacket, with different colours inside and out. Before heading onto a main street, the gloves get stuffed down a sewer grate, along with the blond wig; he now has short black hair.

A nearby convenience store provides the privacy of a bathroom to further transform...the bottoms of the cargo pants get unzipped and removed, so now he's wearing shorts; the pant leg bottoms go in a jacket pocket. The coloured contact lenses get removed and tossed into the toilet, where they easily flush down, along with a much needed piss. Before leaving the bathroom, the cheek implants (removable; often used in acting) come out, and get rolled up in paper towel before going in a pocket. The door he opens with another paper towel, to avoid leaving fingerprints.

He tosses the implants and pant leg bottoms down another sewer grate while heading down another alley, towards a local coffee shop which has some really good muffins; the coffee ain't bad either. Finally, he seats himself in a padded chair, the better to enjoy the tasty treats. As the police comb the area for the "violent offender", none suspect the calm, almost bored looking man in the coffee shop, which is natural enough as he bears zero resemblance at all to the one they seek.

As you can plainly see, a mask would not have been nearly as effective as the multi-layered approach taken by this forward-planning superhero. Let's say, for the sake of argument, that he'd just gone with a mask for identity protection...how would that have worked out? Well, the initial running away would have remained the same, and removal of the mask while on the run would help a goodly bit. However, the rest of the clothing remains the exact same as in the description given to the cops, giving them a much greater chance of catching him.

In addition, the very detailed facial/hair description the witnesses were able to give the police from having seen the intentionally distorted features aided in getting away more easily. With a specific description to check for, the cops were able to have their attention slide right on past the person being searched for, which works perfectly for our purposes. So, with a triumphant example held firmly in mind, let's examine more closely the various things which will help ensure the longevity of your brutal Justice Crusade.

Reversible Jacket: Truly amazing what such a simple item can do in a getaway situation. Simply step around a corner, turn it inside out and **Blam!!** You're a completely different person when viewed from a distance. Especially if the colour shown before or after transformation is particularly vibrant, it'll throw people off the trail pretty damn well. Consider also the fact that often people can only give the vaguest of descriptions, especially if in a high tension situation, and you'll see just how much value this item of clothing can provide.

Coloured Contact Lenses: Look deep into my eyes...for some reason, eyes and eye colour are very important to plenty of folks. Perhaps it's the whole "window into the soul" thing, or whatever, who knows. But although we don't give a flying fuck at a running donkey about *why* people get all gaga about those little round orbs, it gives us another tool to use when trying to remain free to kill all the deserving scum. You see, all you have to do is get a pair of contact lenses in a colour different from your own—preferably vastly different—and people won't recognize you so well without them, especially in conjunction with other disguise strategies.

You can also use some crazy demon, cat or lizard style contacts to play up the horror factor when using a mask. Milky white, all black, or other solid colour versions work well for freak-out potential; get creative. If you aren't having fun while choking the life out of criminals, you're doing it wrong.

Hats: Hats are a simple and versatile way to change your look; that's the reason they have been in fashion for so bloody long. Ever notice how you may not recognize a person you've seen in passing multiple times before, simply because on this occasion they weren't wearing a hat? Because the hat changed the whole look of the entire head, they just weren't immediately recognizable without one.

Use this to your advantage, and take it further even. A wide brimmed hat can block security cameras mounted high up from getting a view of your face. Or how about using a hat associated with another nationality/ethnicity? A sombrero or turban can really throw people off, making it so their description of you to cops points in an entirely different direction. If they're seeking a Sikh, they'll not spot a Greek.

Prosthetics and Movie Make-up: Why fight crime using your everyday face, when it's possible to look completely like someone else? Use the magick of movie make-up techniques to transform like the mysterious chameleon, ever elusive and free. Simple tricks like cheek inserts to hold in the mouth will transform one's entire facial dimensions and look; they'll affect the sound of your speech, too. The look of skin diseases can be duplicated; wrinkles can be added or paved over. A single community college course on the topic would get you to the point of being capable of creating a distorted image which will fool witnesses. Add some facial hair, maybe a stick-on wart...the sky's the limit!

Silicone Masks: For around $800 or so, you can purchase a very realistic silicone face...well, total head covering, actually. Complete with freckles, hair, wrinkles, etcetera, and tight fitting enough for your facial movements to look pretty natural, these enable you to turn completely into another person, even a different race. Matching "sleeve" arm/hand coverings can be purchased for a seamless look. **Con:** Ditching your disguise costs $1600.

Glasses: You know the drill; Clark Kent removes his eyeglasses and transforms into Superman. For some odd reason, no one can recognize the one as being the other...glasses are just that great a disguise. Well, although this is obviously exaggerated, it does contain a useful kernel of truth; eyeglasses and sunglasses do change one's appearance to a certain extent. Just think of that pair of sunglasses that made you look like total shit, or the first time a coworker showed up without their customary eyeglasses and people didn't recognize him at first glance. Yep, there's something to that silly comic book idea after all.

Please don't go out there with just a pair of sunglasses for a disguise when killing meth dealers though; you're gonna end up in prison or the morgue really quickly. What I'm suggesting is to **add** the appearance changing properties of eye or sunglasses to an overall disguise strategy. So remember folks, if you're reading this after a loved one got stabbed to death when crack-heads recognized him from a drug raid while wearing glasses as his sole disguise, it ain't my fault.

Occupational Disguises: This was touched upon before, but merits a more in-depth treatment. It is based on the fact that we live in a society full of people who glide by us without attracting much attention. Just think about it; janitors in office buildings; fast-food workers waiting for busses; painters and window washers going to and from job sites; construction workers complete with fully laden tool belts...it goes on and on. Depending on your mission, choosing to dress as one of these individuals can facilitate mission success.

Why not foil a mugging dressed as a chef? Their uniforms often go over-top of one's normal clothing anyway, making for a much easier getaway transformation; rip off the outer layer and that's pretty much good enough. Or utilize the ubiquitous lunch pail of the hardy construction worker to conceal a really neat magnum revolver; if guns ain't your thing, the tool belt with hammers and screwdrivers is a toolkit of death in the right hands.

Thrift Store Treasures: Did you know that the thrift store is a goldmine for the vigilante needing disposable disguise components? Well it is; check it out. For one thing, it provides footwear options to throw law enforcement off your trail in the form of used shoes and boots. When there is a need to avoid detection at all costs, nothing can be overlooked, and wearing shoes that exhibit someone else's unique wear pattern can make all the difference. A bigger size than is normally worn can be used with the addition of a pair or two of really thick socks. Be warned though; if the wear pattern and size is too different from your own, it can make running away more troublesome. Keep it in mind, and match the gear to the mission as always.

The other thing to do is get a bunch of clothing in just about your size...slightly bigger is great. Then dress in layers when going out there to crush evil, and reap the benefits as the layers can be shed like snake skins as you make your escape. In summer a single extra layer may be all that can be done, while in winter you can have enough layers that not only will the initial witness/security camera footage description be of someone dressed entirely different, the cops will be looking for someone way bigger as well. When combined with other disguise strategies, it can work out awesomely well.

But disguising yourself isn't always enough; sometimes your vehicle of choice needs a disguise as well.
With that in mind, here are some vehicle disguise ideas:

Bogus License Plates: So you've escaped the scene of retribution but unbeknownst to you, a security camera got your license plate. So a cop pulls you over at gunpoint, and the nightmare begins...should have used bogus license plates while in active mission mode, eh? Too late now though...

Yep, the simple act of having a different plate from the one being searched for can keep you free of prison shower ass-raping, and able to continue busting heads in the outside world. The simplest method is to get old license plates, or commandeer (take) some not too long before the mission. A magnetic clip-on system is easy to rig up; put them on your vehicle just prior to entering the mission zone, and remove them shortly after leaving. For a motorcycle, this would be the only way.

For cars, trucks, vans and SUV's, however, a cooler, more James Bond option exists. Plans exist on the internet for how to make a rotating license plate holder, and one with three spots is easy enough to construct. Once installed properly, it allows for changing the license plate being shown at the press of a button; just switch to a bogus plate when entering the action zone, and switch back when leaving. With a third plate to be shown, it allows for even more misdirection! You're at a fucking secret agent level of cool now. ☺

Mud: After the last idea, I feel almost silly mentioning this extremely low-tech idea, but here it is. Slap mud all over your license plate to hide it, then quickly wash it off afterward when making your escape. Sounds kinda lame, but it will work.

Magnetic Stick-on Signs: You'll get away far easier when the cops are looking for a Pizza Hut or Swiss Chalet delivery driver. Whether it's food delivery, a pharmacy service, or a bogus construction company, having a wide variety of vehicle signage will pay off big in the end. Heck, stick a security company logo on your car and match it with a guard uniform along with body armour...get the picture?

That's about it for disguises; if you cannot come up with a workable option from these, it means you have an extreme case of stupidity, and should by no means attempt any vigilante actions. For everyone with a working brain, though, they'll find enough material to work with here, and attain all that their violent daydreams can imagine. Next up, weapons!

{CHAPTER 8} IMPACT WEAPONS...PUTTING THE HURT ON CRIME OLD-SCHOOL!

The comfortably instinctive feel of impact weapons makes them a popular choice for imposing harsh Justice.

The very first weapon ever used by man was an impact weapon. Whether it was a big stick, a rock, or an animal bone that was lying around, mankind knew a good thing when they saw it. It was superior to using one's hand in so many ways; it hits harder; it can give more reach; it saves one's hands from those fucking annoying broken bones; most importantly though, it's really, really fun.

Now sure, it's not politically correct to say so, but we're violent vigilantes...we don't give a shit about politically correct bull-crap! Besides, even the weakling, brain-washed masses know in the deepest parts of their souls that this is the truth. The only reason you can get people to play a game as mind-bogglingly dull as baseball or golf is the momentary joy inherent to bashing something with a stick. Same goes for hockey and lacrosse, where they are even more honest about it and at least use their sticks to ram into each other; long live brutality!

Baseball Bats: Nothing else can compare to a solid wood baseball bat for sheer exuberant, evil-bashing fun. Indeed, the only reason anyone bothers to play or watch baseball is likely as an alibi for lugging one of these bludgeons around in the trunk of their car. Upon picking one up and taking a tentative swing with it, one feels an immediate connection with our caveman ancestors, and the urge to bash open a skull comes on with force. With good reach, great bashing power, plausible deniability when carrying it and immense ease of use, there's almost no down side.

In fact, the only down side would be if you're planning on mainly being a foot patrol/motorcycle/bike or skateboard hero...in that case there would be a hard time carrying or explaining it. In the trunk of one's car along with a catcher's mitt, it is perfectly innocuous; when carrying it slung over the shoulder in an alley while dressed all in black, however, it's going to be classified as a deadly weapon. Get one anyway though, as at some point you'll doubtlessly find a use for it.

Extendable Batons: A new favourite for police forces and security guards around the world, extendable batons provide scum-smashing power in a compact package. Although cheap brands abound, it's best to invest in a higher quality one; ASP and Monadnock are two of the biggest brand names in that market, and most cops go with one of those. They are available in lengths ranging from 12 to 26 inches extended length, and the shorter ones can be found with a handy pocket-clip for ease of carry.

In order to stay open, a couple of mechanisms are employed. The oldest and most inexpensive is the friction lock variety: each tube is flared bigger towards the back and crimped down towards the front, making it so the whole assembly locks into place with friction when snapped open forcefully. In order to close it, one must impact the tip into something solid, like concrete or the floor. The other system can be snapped or pulled into position, and is then released with the push of a button, or twisting the rods in a specific way, disengaging the locking mechanism. There are a few different proprietary mechanisms used for this purpose by each company, and their literature will explain the specifics more fully.

Choice of length is entirely up to each hero, but 21 inches has proven to be pretty darned good for being concealable, while still having enough bashing power. For those wanting big bashing power in a smaller package though, I have the answer you need. First off, choose a friction lock model in the 12-16 inch length; then, unscrew the butt-cap, and remove the little clip that holds the tubes immobile when closed. After that, fill the striking tube with lead...it is up to you whether to just jam in some lead slugs (available from shooting reloading supplies stores), or to melt some lead and pour it in. To melt, all you need is a stove/hot plate and a steel pot; wheel weights work as a lead source, although you'll have to skim off the gunk which floats to the top. Have good ventilation for the toxic fumes. I recommend using a steel funnel to direct the lead neatly in, ensuring the action remains free of spills. Another option some use is to file some lead into filings, then mix them with epoxy. Pour the epoxy & lead mixture into the striking tube; it will harden into a sturdy weight.

They can be very effective as long as you ignore ALL police and security training/methodology as to their use. Hit every target *they* tell you not to: the head, the neck, the wrists and elbows...pretty much any bony area. The cops are told to aim for large muscle groups in the interests of avoiding lawsuits for lethal force. One problem though, which is that those strikes don't work worth shit, so you have to keep bashing for little to no real effect. We don't mind if the evildoer dies, particularly, so bash that fucker in the head with a lead-weighted ASP and watch him hit the ground hard.

Saps and Blackjacks: These snazzy little bashers were a mainstay of street-level law enforcement for a very long time, so much so that police pants had a special pocket in them to carry a flat sap. A blackjack would also sort of fit in that pocket, or might be in a pouch on the belt. Because they worked so well, thugs decided that they too could make use of them, which led to today's situation where they are banned in certain locations, demonized as a "weapon of the lower classes." They aren't carried so much anymore...

But you can bring it back! The old technology still works great, and allows—indeed, requires—one to get right in there toe-to-toe and still have power to knock them senseless, into unconsciousness or death (depending on the type and size used, among other factors). Let's look at what they are exactly:

Both saps and blackjacks use lead or steel to provide the bashing weight. Blackjacks have a coil spring in the handle, and flat saps can be built with a flat spring in theirs. The blackjack uses a solid striking weight; saps can be made with solid metal weights, or by filling them with lead or steel shot. Saps also come in two varieties, hard and soft; soft is better for knocking people out, whereas hard is better for eliminating them from the gene pool. Saps generally have designated striking surfaces, although the flat variety can deliver more concentrated strikes with its edge; it will suffer damage over time that way, though, and may fail at the wrong moment. Just hit with the correct part, eh? Blackjacks offer a 360 degree striking surface, as they are totally round.

Palm saps are available in hard and soft versions also, and are held in the palm, with a strap that goes around the back of the hand. At night, or if one were wearing gloves the same colour as the sap, it would appear that you could knock someone out or possibly kill them with nothing more than a slap; that'll build a wicked reputation in a hurry. ☺

Golf Clubs/Hockey Sticks/Lacrosse Sticks: All weapons of last resort; they're too big for the amount of damage infliction potential. They work better than nothing and do provide distance, but use just about anything else.

Cricket Bats: Reference the baseball bat section above; cricket bats will work out just about as well, and can also be an inconspicuous trunk/backseat weapon. Leave it in the car at all times to be ready for a jolly old shit-kicking adventure.

The Club: That stupid anti-theft device people stick on their steering wheel. It won't stop a determined thief, but it **does** pull apart into two very sturdy, incredibly handy steel bashing devices! Completely normal to have in the passenger compartment of the car (might as well have one to use...they do deter lazy thieves), it is ready for action in the blink of an eye, and people just don't seem to see it coming.

Hammers: These tools range in size from tiny tack hammers and brass ones for precise tapping adjustments, all the way up to five-foot war hammers and sledgehammers. A size exists to meet all your specific needs, even the crime-fighting ones. A solid choice is actually a rock pick, as it has a striking face and a spike on the back; it's made for picking and cracking rocks, but it'll crack a skull just as well. If hammers turn out to really be your thing, consider taking a war hammer and shortening the haft so that it can be used in closer quarters. Leave some reach, but limber it up...you ain't fighting marauders on horseback here. However, if for some odd reason you find yourself needing to fight a gang of psycho motorcycle bandits who charge into battle mounted on their steel steeds—hey, it could happen—then a full length war hammer would be just the ticket.

Short handled sledgehammers will come in handy for motorcycle based "carjacking" scenarios, as well as for breaking bones during interrogations. Generic looking ones complete with a patina of use will work great on a tool-belt when disguised as a construction worker or handyman sort. Point is that they are versatile, coming in a wide range of sizes, shapes and configurations, enough to fulfill many mission roles. You *need* to have some hammers in your bag of tricks.

Crowbars: A solid chunk of steel upside the head will handily adjust the attitude of any criminal. They're also great for prying your way into places you aren't necessarily allowed. Pry that nailed-up abandoned building open, and go kill the junky scum hiding within its depths! A compact version will fit easily into a backpack.

Brass Knuckles: Popular with brutal thugs around the world, these babies have also been used by soldiers, bodyguards, and many others who needed more *"Oomph!"* in their hits. With a multitude of styles, you can get variants with one, two, three or four finger holes.

Finger holes may be round or oval, with most knowledgeable folks preferring oval; it's just a better fit for smashing things in comfort. Some are blunt over the knuckles, while others tend to have spiky or bumpy protrusions. Depending on the style selected, they may also add damage to hammer-fist and top of hand strikes. Materials used include brass; steel; aluminum; titanium; lead; wood; Micarta; G-10 and assorted high-impact plastics. Interesting fun fact: the non-metal variants are legal to own in Canada and most of the USA, making them a possible choice for when having completely illegal items would be a liability.

Whack-ball of Death: This one is a personal favourite, and is so elegantly simple yet deadly. Simply take a 2 to 2.5 inch diameter steel ball bearing and place it in a hood cut from one of those hooded sweat-shirts (or "Hoodies"...hate that fucking name). Then just grip the hood so the bottom is closed, and the ball bearing is contained. After that, simply bash someone in the head at anywhere close to full force, and they'll die. It's pretty much the best close-quarter's murder weapon you'll come across; silent, deadly, and easily disposable (the bloody hood just gets tossed or burned; the ball bearing can be tossed in a river if so desired). Don't be surprised if you keep finding yourself using this little bad boy again and again over the years.

Alright then, that's enough to get the impact weapon train rolling. By exploring what these have to offer, you will discover the fundamentals of impact weapons, and can start figuring which ones to include on your missions into the heart of darkness. May they serve you well, as they have countless generations of your ancestors. Full-steam ahead now though, for we go to examine mankind's second oldest weapons; blades and pointy things.

{CHAPTER 9} "DID YOU EVER DREAM YOU HAVE CLAWS?" KNIVES, SPEARS AND OTHER SHARP THINGS

Humans are a strange breed of animal; not only do we lack a shell or tough, armoured skin, nature has ill equipped us in the offensive department as well. Born into this world with no claws and a mouth full of rather blunt teeth, mankind's deficiencies were painfully obvious once competition with dedicated predators was started. Tigers can run faster, bite harder, and tear us into little scraps with their nasty claws. Whether we went up against lions, hyenas, crocodiles or even baboons, the losing side was ours...in the beginning, at least. For humans are strange animals in another way as well; we have a totally bitchin brain in our arsenal.

So we decided to stop with the creature feature envy, and proceeded to equip ourselves with those things nature had denied unto us. From the first time some clumsy cave-dude cut himself with a sharp rock, it was full-steam ahead in the sharp implements arms race. Beginning with sharp shards of broken rock, the ability to cut flesh from the animals we scavenged was gained. Beginning with the first pointy stick or piece of antler humans stabbed something—perhaps each other—with, it was clear that they were onto something. When some guy lost to the mists of time grabbed the lower jawbone of an animal and smashed in the skull of another creature, the axe was on its way to being born.

Rocks began to be deliberately shaped; more suitable rocks were discovered, like flint or obsidian; skills like knapping became a vital part of the human survival toolkit. Copper ore was discovered, probably from rocks in or surrounding an ancient camp fire; learning to shape by moulding and pounding/hammering was next. From there came bronze (tin and copper combined); iron ore was discovered...someone discovered steel when carbon got introduced into the iron mix somehow. Alongside the developing stone and then metallurgical side of things, humans came up with specific tool variants to better utilize them, and to accomplish specific tasks. Knives, swords, spears, axes, pole-arms, all these things developed into their own unique categories, and within each category huge variations abounded as well.

Which brings us to now, brave reader, a time in which a bewildering variety of edged weapons and tools are yours for the choosing. Steel varieties up the wazoo; titanium alloys and ceramics; what is a newcomer to the field to make of all this choice? Don't fret though, for I am here to guide you along the correct path, providing the information required to make the proper choices to maximize mission effectiveness while minimizing unnecessary outlay of cash.

Knives:

With a wide assortment of shapes and sizes, there's a knife to suit all your crime-fighting needs. ☺

At the most basic level, knives are split into two categories: **fixed blade** knives, and **folding** knives. Fixed blade knives are carried in a sheath which covers the blade, whereas folding knives fold so that the blade is safely covered by the handle itself. This also means that on a folding knife, the blade will always be shorter than the handle. Folding knives can be carried loose in a pocket, in a belt sheath/pouch, or held in place with a pocket clip. The pocket clip gives the best option for speed of deployment, especially because the knife will be held in the same position—place and orientation—every single time. Popular carry spots with clips include front or rear pocket; in the waistband of pants; some people clip one into the top of their boot. Others carry in odd ways such as using a wrist/forearm strap which the clip can latch onto, allowing it to be carried in a sleeve; the same can be done with a suitably sized fixed blade knife.

A multitude of blade shapes are available in each. There is hawkbill (curved/claw); sheepsfoot (blunt); clip point; wharncliffe; drop point; trailing point (looks like a Persian scimitar shape); Tanto; reverse Tanto; kris (wavy); spear point; dagger...and a bunch of mixtures of those basic shapes. There are also swedges, which is a feature of the blade near the tip. It looks almost like an edge is being ground there; it reduces weight and facilitates penetration, depending on how it is done. Sometimes it is fully sharpened, making a short length of double edge. Double edged blades allow for cutting in both directions and add stabbing power, but are generally limited to fixed blades, as very few folding knives have a handle which completely covers the entire blade including both sides. Let's look a little closer at each main category now.

Folding Knives: There are locking and non-locking/slip-joint style folding knives. Some have a single blade while others have many; in general, the crime-fighting superhero will want a locking folder with a single blade. Non-locking folders can be good for utility, especially if they have a multitude of different blades, but suck giant donkey dicks when it comes to combative use. For stabbing folks and dealing with the unpredictable angles of force involved in the chaos of battle, you need to have a blade which locks.

Not only that, but you need a reliable lock that is strong enough. The AXIS, compression, Tri-Ad and regular back-lock are among the strongest, although a properly made balisong knife with hefty pivot pins will offer the ultimate in avoiding having it close on your hand...it is illegal merely to own in many places though. Liner-locks and frame-locks are strong enough if made well, but the frame-lock offers more safety for heroic use, as your hand actually prevents lock slippage as you grip the handle (your grip keeps the lock-bar engaged rather than being free to move at all).

Different methods of opening a folder exist, including the good old-fashioned nail-nick for a two-handed opening. However, we'll be looking at one-hand opening methods here, as speed is of the essence. Thumb studs, thumb holes, and thumb disks; all give a spot for your thumb to "grab" the blade, allowing you to then open the knife. Assisted opening knives have a spring which *assists* in opening the blade once it opens to 30 degrees; some knives use thumb studs or disks for the initial opening, while others use a *flipper*. A flipper is a protrusion from the base of the blade which juts out the back of the handle slightly when closed; one pushes on the protrusion to open the knife. The flipper is also found on many unassisted knives, and if it is prominent enough—like on the Zero Tolerance 0561—it acts as an additional safety device, as your hand cannot slide onto the blade, nor can the blade close on your fingers if the lock fails. Switchblade/automatic knives use a spring which is activated at the push of a button to open, and are illegal lots of places; often they use a button-lock, which is another strong lock available on some non-auto knives as well.

Fixed Blade Knives: With fixed blades knives, the steel which extends into or through the handle is called the *tang*. Full-tang knives have the steel extend the full length of the handle, with slab sided handle scales for grip (made of G-10, Micarta, stag, rubber, wood, carbon fiber, etc.). Sometimes holes are drilled or material is milled out of the tang in order to reduce weight, but this can lead to failure points resulting in breakage; a full tang with no cutouts will be strongest. The full-tang can be tapered towards the back in order to affect balance or weight without weakening it nearly so much.

Rat-tail tangs, partial tangs and hidden tangs all pass into or through the handle. A rat-tail tang narrows down a bunch and extends out the back of the handle, where it is peened in place or secured with a pommel nut. Partial tangs can extend anywhere from barely in to nearly out the back; they are either moulded-on or held in place with super-strong epoxies generally. Hidden tangs are much like partial except for usually extending almost the whole length of the handle, with some having a screw coming from the butt of the handle into a threaded section of the tang. People can and do argue semantics, and there are a few more variations...but fuck it, this is enough to run with!

Generally, you are going to want a full-tang fixed blade; the style and length of blade will depend on the mission, concealment needs, and what it needs to do (utility or killing?). Any less than 2 inches, and why bother. Once you get past 12 inches of blade, then it actually begins to get classified as a short sword.

Kydex sheaths will probably work best for most needs, although leather is classic and looks good. Kydex is a tough thermo-plastic, often used in making knife sheaths; it will not retain water, and can be fully washed out afterward to get rid of any icky blood residue from your enthusiastic scum removal activities. Zytel and other moulded plastics are used in making sheaths too.

Steel: You can get anything from totally corrosion resistant H1 steel (can be left in saltwater for years with no rust), to super edge-retaining CPM-S110V, to mega tough CPM-3V. 5160 steel is used in truck leaf springs, and will make a knife which will take a beating too. Just remember this: **titanium is a terrible choice for a knife blade!** I know, it sounds all space-tastic, and Blade used it in his movies, but it does not harden like steel, nowhere close in fact. The only thing it's great for is corrosion resistance and being non-magnetic, but unless you're defusing land mines or some other specific thing that needs it, don't bother.

Swords:

***Even cats recognize the value of a
good sword, machete, or axe.***

Swords are bigger than knives, and better for a battlefield...they tend to get noticed while walking downtown in major urban centers, though. Even on actual battlefields these days, swords are far less prevalent than in years gone by, although the modern tactical sword has made its way out there, racking up a body count in a sphere normally dominated by guns, bombs, and heavy air support.

We'll split swords first into one-handed and two-handed, along with the bastard-type which is hand-and-a-half. A two-handed sword can be gripped with two hands (obviously), although shorter varieties can be wielded with one hand at a slight loss of finesse and speed. One-handed swords tend to be shorter than two-handed versions, but some old sabers are just as long as a two-handed katana. In general though, two-handed swords are long, and one-handed swords are short. Hand-and-a-half can be either length, but are generally somewhere in the middle; the slightly longer handle allows for a second hand to get about a 3-finger grip in order to add force or speed of redirection.

The modern crime-fighter will generally be going with a one-handed sword with no more than a 20-inch blade...a Wakizashi or Gladius will do you more good on the mean streets than a Claymore with an overall length of 55 inches (4.5 feet and a bit; slightly hard to conceal). Just stay away from anything advertised as having a stainless steel blade...it will break; it's only a matter of when. Go with blades made of carbon steels like 1080, 1070, 5160, CPM-3V. Some manufacturers even use 1050 or 1060 to good effect, and the cost will be less for materials. Do your research and be prepared to spend a fair chunk of cash to get something that will fit all your exacting requirements.

Machetes:

The true workhorse of the knife-related world, machetes come in many shapes and sizes. Ones for clearing the jungle in South America evolved from Cutlasses, and when you need to get through that damned undergrowth, nothing else will do. Other variants look like cleavers, overgrown knives, mutated swords, and all sorts of shapes that work really well for their intended purposes, but defy description. Many hard-working people around the world do everything with them, from cutting wood/clearing trails to preparing food for dinner...they'll serve you well.

Available in thicknesses ranging from 0.0625 to 0.250-inch thickness depending on intended use, there is a size and shape perfectly suited to any conceivable heroic need. The crime-fighter in an urban setting will likely want no more than a 12-inch blade version, as it can be shoved in a pack or hidden under a trench coat. Something in a thickness of 0.187 to 0.250 of an inch will do; 0.125-inch-thick can work, but lacks that *"Oomph!"* which one might really want. Lop that arm right off of the next scum-rot savage that crosses your path!

Spears:

They sure worked well for the Zulus...
Simply a stick with a point, spears have been responsible for more deaths in combat than probably any other weapon ever. Even once metallurgy got going really well, the amount of steel on the end of a

spear was more economical than a sword, and in a group setting makes a better fighting formation. The Zulus kicked serious ass in southern Africa, forging an empire at the point of their spears. They shortened the shaft and used a bigger blade, which, combined with intensive fighting training, proved totally awesome. Their Assegai worked well in the close-up, brutal battles they excelled in...why not do the same?

Yep, I'm saying you should get yourself an Assegai and go stab the shit right out of some crack-heads as soon as possible. They won't know what the fuck gives as you charge right in there with a gut-wrenching, fear-inducing battle cry and open their throats in a shower of gore.

People still know the name of Shaka Zulu; make your name resound through the ages as well.

Axes:

Get the power of fear on your side. The Axe Murderer has become such an ingrained part of our cultural psyche, and all that fear can be put to good use by the proper person...you *are* the proper person, right?

Axes range in size from one-pound hatchets all the way up to eight-pound splitting mauls. Battle axes tended to range between one to six pounds, depending on length and whether they were to be wielded with one or two hands. Replica battle axes can still be purchased, and some truly are ready for brutal use. In general though, you're going to want something of a modern design. How about a nice full-tang tomahawk with G-10 handles and a spike on the back? Or why not put an Estwing camping axe in the back seat of your car? As long as you buy quality products, it will be more up to how it goes with the overall look being aimed for; battle-ready commando, or psycho woodsman on a rampage? They both have unique fear points in their favour. ☺

Pole-arms: Basically they are metal blades and such on the end of a long stick. Long blades over a foot long, axe heads, hammers with spikes...there's a lot of variation within the category. An English Billhook looks a lot different than a Japanese Naginata, but they'll both work against a guy charging on horseback, which is what they were used for a bunch. Clippity-clop, clippity-clop, **poleaxe in the face!**

Cheap to make due to maximizing the weapon mileage for amount of metal used, they were popular with peasant classes, and were often improvised/modified from agricultural implements and other tools. With big angular momentum, spiked varieties could pierce plate armour, opening knights like a tin can. In the modern world, they'll be difficult to lug around without getting hassled, but if you want to knock gang members off their motorcycles as they charge wildly at you, a pole-arm might be just the thing.

Suppliers:

Folding Knives: Good ones to buy from are Spyderco; Emerson; Benchmade; Zero Tolerance/Kershaw; Chris Reeve Knives; Strider; Cold Steel; Buck Knives

Fixed Blade Knives: Buy from ESEE Knives; Busse Combat; Ontario Knives; Cold Steel; Condor Knife and Tool; Bark River Knife and Tool; Buck Knives; TOPS Knives

Machetes: Condor Knife and Tool; Imacassa; Cold Steel; Tramontina; Ontario Knives

Axes/Tomahawks: Get them from Wetterlings; Condor Knife and Tool; Gransfors Bruk; Cold Steel; Estwing; Winkler Knives; RMJ Tactical

Swords: Cas Iberia; Cold Steel; Hanwei; Kingdom Armory; Windlass Steelcrafts; Condor Knife and Tool

Cold Steel deserves a section of its own; no one respects your decision to become a violent, crime-fighting vigilante the way they do! They have weaponry to fill many of your brutal weapon needs. Folding knives with nigh on indestructible locks; machetes of almost every shape and size; swords big enough to satisfy Conan the Barbarian; shuriken, throwing knives and sturdy (yet cheap enough to throw away) sword canes round things out, with even more options all the time. Where else can you buy a war hammer, a sword cane, *and* a knife accurately marketed as a folding sword? They have blowguns too.

To help get you up to speed, Cold Steel also offers training DVDs to brush up on your armed and unarmed skills...why not watch them instead of infomercials in the wee hours of the morning when your fierce thirst for vengeance keeps sleep at bay? Training versions for much of their product line are available.

For bringing harsh Justice into places guarded by metal detectors, use one of their fiberglass reinforced nylon knives. Their weirder offerings—such as the sjambok—will work great in your torture room.

Just remember not to bring a knife or sword to a gunfight; well, I guess you *can* if you armour up enough, and just want an extra level of challenge. In general though, it's better to even the odds in your favour, so strap yourself in and get ready to enter the wonderful world of guns!

{CHAPTER 10} GUNS: A BARREL FULL OF FUN

Choosing the correct firearm can
make your entire outfit pop!

Guns get a bad rap from many wimpy segments of society, and have even been vilified by certain vigilantes who should know better. For some reason, an idea persists that *real men* settle things with their fists, and that somehow beating someone to death with a club or stabbing them 57 times with a sword is more *civilized* or *romantic*.

What a load of rhinoceros' ball-sucking tripe! The dweebs detached from reality I can forgive, but the crime-fighters are deluding themselves if they think that a head smacked with a crowbar is somehow more civilized; ever see the splatter pattern of brains on a back-alley brick wall? It ain't pretty. How about a corpse with 35 stab and slash wounds...yuck!

Now this isn't to say that an exit wound is a pretty sight, because it most assuredly ain't; however, it is no worse, and those who eschew the use of firearms for such idiotic reasons are missing out on a fantastic evil elimination device. Besides, shooting things with guns is fun. ☺

"What?" you exclaim in bewilderment; "You just went on about the horrific nature of deadly trauma, and you're talking about **fun?**" Yep, I sure am, and not only are guns fun, they open up a whole new realm of coolness, too. Besides, we're killing **evil people**, so you really need to get the proper mindset towards the whole endeavor. So sit back, chill the fuck out, and check out this instructive scenario to get you on the right page:

A lone figure sits hidden on a rooftop in the night, peering out into the gloom which enfolds the city. No one calls this building home anymore; as jobs left the area, so did many of the people. Some folks couldn't afford to leave from the area entirely though, whether due to lack of money and opportunity or because of strong ties to family. Then again, some people are just plain stubborn and refuse to let circumstance dictate what their actions will be...foolish or brave, they remain all the same. It is for these souls that the shrouded figure on the roof maintains a watchful vigil.

The heroic defender of this region peers into the night with a combination of binoculars and a night vision device, as lighting is sporadic due to electricity cut-backs by the city. There are also a few directional microphones set up to capture sounds of villainy from multiple angles. He has set up a hunting blind of sorts high above the mean streets; the junk left behind when the building was abandoned makes it easy to build a hiding spot out of assorted refuse, scraps of fabric and some camouflage netting. This hunter is not seeking deer though, oh no, he is hunting the most dangerous of game; humans who have turned against their fellow man.

One of the directional microphones detects commotion off towards the east...time to get a visual on it. Powerful binoculars get the scene into focus, and the staunch hero is not surprised at what they show; a gang of fuck-faced assholes has decided to rob a couple out for a nice romantic walk in the night. Given what he knows about the savages in this area, it's pretty much a sure bet that they'll add a bit of the old raping into the mix, making the guy watch before beating them to unconsciousness or death. Yep, one of them is now grabbing the girl and pulling her off towards the nearest alley.

Cold rage builds in his chest, and he grimly swears "Not tonight, assholes!" as he sets aside the binoculars and grabs the carbine. For this type of job, he has selected a bolt-action carbine firing a .45 caliber ACP round; the set-up is complete with a silencer (suppressor, for all you terminology nuts) and a 20 times magnification scope. It's a bit more magnification than is strictly required, but allows him to see the expression on the scummy bastard's face as he sends a sub-sonic lead slug crashing through the center of it. Blood splatters the girl, but she's too much in shock to notice the blood of her would-be rapist; she just freezes in place.

The other 3 guys don't freeze, however, but they have no clue that death has come for them from above! With comical ineffectiveness they pull out guns, knives, or duck behind nearby cars. This saves them not at all though, for the firing angle the roof provides negates the cover they think such things provide. As bullets fly through the night with a quiet "thwip", Justice is brought to the night-time streets yet again. The couple gets the hell out of there as the last body hits the ground, just glad to be alive. Placing the gun down beside him, the triumphant vigilante blows out a slow breath, and takes a sip of his coffee. Given what he knows about police response in this area, there will be plenty of time to go down and toss those jerks in a convenient dumpster. In a flash of artistic inspiration, the decision is made to mark the scene with a local gang's graffiti tags; that way, if the cops actually get off their fat asses and investigate for a change, it will put the heat on another grouping of useless low-lifes.

With a spring in his step and a happy tune to whistle, the descent down to ground level commences. Tonight's hunting was productive, and it always feels good to make a difference.

Wow, silently saving the day while cloaked in total anonymity; a perfect operation all around. Like the hand of a vengeful god he struck the evildoers down without them having the slightest hope of escape, nor were they given the chance to use either of their intended victims as hostages in an attempt to escape retribution. By combining sound tactics with the proper equipment, this individual was able to balance the scales of Justice in style. Admit it, you cheered when rapist boy got hot lead through his face; well, the same power can be at your fingertips too.

So, with that all settled, let's get down to basics. I'll provide you the data you need to find the correct level to firepower to take your fight against crime to the next level. There's a bunch to learn, so put a pot of coffee on, get settled in a comfy chair, and I'll download the goods straight to your brain.

The Basics:

We'll be sticking with modern weaponry here, so forget about wheel-locks, matchlocks, flintlocks, muskets and other old-timey stuff. Thus we'll start with the most basic divisions: **handguns; rifles; carbines; shotguns; sub-machineguns and machineguns.**

Handguns: These include revolvers; semi-automatic pistols; as well as single, double, or weird variants like four barreled pistols. Size can range from tiny Derringers a few inches long all the way up to huge honkin magnum revolvers with 14 inch barrels. Single-action revolvers need to have the hammer cocked each time before pulling the trigger; double-action revolvers fire each time the trigger is pulled, although most can be cocked for an easier trigger pull; double-action only revolvers cannot be cocked.

Semi-auto pistols can be single action, in which case it must be cocked before being able to fire the first time, after which each pull of the trigger fires a round; double-action ones can have the first round fired just by pulling the trigger, although with a heavier trigger tension, after which they have the same trigger pull as a single-action does on subsequent shots. Just as with revolvers, there exist double-action only versions, where the trigger tension is the same each and every time.

Single, double or four barrel pistols are break-open action by design; the barrel hinges away from the handle, and you put a round in each chamber before closing. Some have a single hammer, whereas others have multiple ones. You cock each time you wish to shoot; some double barrel pistols have two triggers, so both hammers could be cocked at the same time in order to provide a quick follow-up shot.

Rifles: Far better for long-range evil elimination operations. These firearms generally use a far larger amount of gunpowder than handguns, and operate at higher pressures, allowing for greater projectile speed. This faster bullet will have longer range and a flatter trajectory, meaning you don't have to compensate for how far the bullet drops as it slows quite so much at medium ranges; at long range, ballistics becomes a real factor. Rifles generally come in bolt-action; semi-automatic; single shot break-action (although there are a few double barrel rifles out there); lever-action, and even pump-action. There are also full-auto rifles for military use, which generally have a selector switch for semi-auto, full-auto, or 3-round burst (each pull of the trigger fires three rounds).

Ammo capacity for rifles varies greatly, all the way from a single shot break-action, up to a 50 round drum magazine attached to a full-auto capable assault rifle. Unless you're commandeering gear from a local military armoury, though, 10 to 30 rounds is not an unreasonable expectation capacity-wise, and will work just fine for most crime-busting needs.

Carbines: Carbines are just rifles that use handgun ammunition. The benefit to you as a vigilante could be the ability to use the same ammunition in your handgun and rifle, or the fact that sub-sonic rounds capable of being effectively silenced become an option. Some carbines use a revolver mechanism; all the other types used in rifles are used in carbines as well.

Shotguns: Is there any firearm more versatile than the humble shotgun? With a simple change of ammunition (and possibly a choke tube) one can switch from shooting birds, to deer, all the way up to bears and Cape Buffalo. Available in single or double barrel, semi-auto, bolt-action and pump-action variants, shotguns are easily available around the world, as is much of their ammunition. As well, people all around the world, from the plains of Africa to the streets of Moscow, they all understand the simple, universal language of a

12-gauge barrel pointed at their face. When you have firepower of this magnitude, communication is easy.

Sub-machineguns: Compact firearms with full-auto capability. Utilizing handgun ammunition, a sub-machinegun is great for slaughtering crime in enclosed spaces. Just go easy on that trigger... you can burn through a full mag in double-quick time. With the choice of sub-sonic ammunition, you can silence a sub-machinegun rather well; don't disturb the neighbours whilst clearing out a home full of scum.

Machineguns: These are the big boys in the automatic weapons game. Ranging in size from oversized rifles to behemoths mounted on the back of a truck, when you need firepower enough to slaughter a village, nothing else will do. Full-sized machineguns are not light, however, so unless you're a 300-pound muscle-monster, it'll be a case of setting it up and blasting from that position (well, you could mount it facing out of a vehicle for the ultimate Justice drive-by).

Ammo can be fed in by big-ass magazines, or with a belt-feed for sustained firing. No matter how much is brought, though, a machinegun eats through your ammo supply faster than many would expect.

Ammunition Choices:

So you've tentatively decided on a gun which seems to fit in with your unique hero style and mission intent; that must mean you're ready to rock, right?

No, it does not, for there is the not so little choice of ammunition. The NRA likes to say that guns don't kill people, people do...if they were being fully correct, the actual truth is that bullets kill people (unless you cave in a skull with your gun or skewer them with a bayonet...). With this in mind, let's take a look at various ammo choices and what they bring to the retribution table. ☺

Round-nosed Lead Bullets: An old time favourite, these traditional-style bullets still do fine for attitude adjustment purposes in the modern world. They cannot be used in high-velocity rifles and such, but they'll suffice for most handgun and carbine loads; even some magnum loads are possible with hard-cast lead bullets. Plenty of people around the world can attest to their effectiveness...or could if they weren't long dead and eaten by worms, that is.

Copper-jacketed Bullets: These can be a full metal jacket, where the copper covers the front and sides (but not the back, generally); Soft-nosed jacketed, where the rear and sides are covered, but the front/nose is exposed lead; they can also be hollow-point, where the nose is exposed lead with a "crater" or hole formed in it. The copper jacket allows for use in higher velocity rounds, where all-lead would foul the rifling and just generally fuck things up. The soft-nosed variety is often used for hunting, as it remains aerodynamic in flight, while still expanding nicely inside the body to create a much bigger wound. Hollow-points will be discussed separately.

Hollow-point bullets: They can be either copper jacketed on the side and rear, or made entirely of lead. The hole formed in the nose causes the bullet to dramatically expand in size while passing through the body, causing massive internal damage; this can improve stopping power and lethality, which may be a consideration when imposing your will violently on the criminal world.

Teflon-coated Bullets: These are for defeating Kevlar body armour; however, a more powerful gun will defeat body armour as well. I recommend you just use a more powerful gun if defeating body armour is a big concern for you.

Armour-piercing Bullets: These snazzy bullets have a *penetrator* at their core, made of tungsten, tungsten carbide or some form of hardened steel. The copper casing squishes upon impact, but the fast-moving piece of hardened material should penetrate what you're shooting at. At some point this type of ammo will probably come in handy, although you'll likely have to make your own due to not being a readily bought item.

Shotgun-specific Ammo Choices: The humble shotgun needs a category of its own due to being so fucking versatile. You can always buy various shot shells at any gun store and many hardware stores as well. Buckshot is almost as easily found, and is simply a bigger diameter of lead/steel/bismuth shot which fills the projectile portion of the shotgun shell. Slugs are just big-ass lead bullets, basically, although some are smaller diameter than the actual barrel, and use a plastic sabot to make up the difference; this allows that smaller diameter slug to be shot at much higher velocity (the slug is often a copper-jacketed one in a sabot shell). Sabot slugs may be full metal jacket, hollow-point, all-lead, soft-nose, or a hollow-point with a plastic insert to improve aerodynamics.

Flechette shells are an exotic anti-personnel round, where the shell contains a multitude of little steel darts. Although you'll likely never find any for sale anywhere legally, you can easily make it yourself by loading shells with as many of those little finishing nails as will fit inside. If you don't have reloading equipment, simply pry open the front of the shell, pour out the shot, and replace it with finishing nails. Then just re-crimp the front as best you can and voila!

Silencers:

In the interests of brevity, this will be a short(ish) section. Silencers/suppressors work by keeping all that expanding gas blasting out the front of the barrel contained. The silencer at its most basic is an expansion chamber that holds that gas while the bullet goes along its merry way. Many different methods have been devised to do this, and the internet will provide in-depth information on most of them, along with handy tutorials on how to build such things

If you do not use sub-sonic ammo, the bullet itself will make noise from the sonic boom as it zips along. The good old .22 short and .45 ACP rounds are handily sub-sonic, so they're good choices for such things. The .45 will kill crooks dead more effectively, but will require a far larger silencer due to the **much** larger volume of gas.

For the ultimate easy to install, cheap to throw away silencer, start with a Ruger Mark 2 semi-auto pistol in .22 caliber. File off the front sight; wrap it in some electrical tape, and press-fit a ¾ inch PVC male adapter onto the end of the barrel. This allows for easily screwing various silencers made from common plumbing parts—and possibly aluminum cans—onto it. An easily concealable one is simply a Clog Buster...you just screw a Clog Buster onto that PVC adapter, and you're ready to go out and become the silent death which strikes from shadowy concealment.

Well, we've come a long way so far; you know your hero type; have a name; outfit/armour has been selected; vehicle options have been chosen; plus some disguise options and a wide range of death-dealing weaponry to augment your burgeoning martial arts skills. Or at least you will once you can afford it all...let's switch gears for a bit and check out how you'll be paying for all this snazzy stuff.

{CHAPTER 11} FINANCING THE CRUSADE

Unless you've recently won a few lotteries, all that goes into enthusiastically fighting crime at the highest level possible may seem out of reach. Even if you are one of the fortunate individuals to have a secure, high-paying job in these difficult times, other financial demands likely impinge upon the discretionary funds for such ventures. How will you explain to the wife where the money for that dream vacation in Aruba went, right? Little Billy will be pretty fucking pissed off if his college fund went to pay for body armour and an SUV equipped with forward mounted machineguns. Explaining those sorts of expenses just isn't an option for most folks.

Now I realize that this may not be a concern for all hero types, naturally. If you're the sort of hero who enjoys the minimalistic approach, funding likely won't be an issue. Those who prefer tackling evil with nothing more than a ski mask, leather jacket and an extendable baton will have a pretty damn easy time affording it; however, even those purists will benefit from larger funds behind the enterprise.

Just consider this for a moment; how many more heads could you crack with an extra 40 to 55 hours a week added to the crime-fighting effort? Or what about crime in other provinces/states, other countries even? If you had extra funds and the freedom of scheduling to employ it, who would you be beating right now, and on what continent? Think about it!

I'll start with the idea that the prospective superhero is starting out with low cash flow, and wants to eventually rise to the highest heights of crime-fighting success. Okay, then, the first thing to do is get at least the bare minimum of gear required, which would be something along the lines of a hunting balaclava, thrift store clothing, cut-resistant gloves and a club of some sort. The exact specifics can vary, but some means of maintaining anonymity and a weapon of some form aren't really negotiable. A few months of martial arts and getting in shape would be a good idea as well; remember what happened in the example of the guy who didn't learn how to fight before setting out on the road to brutal adventuring. At the very least you'll need to get fit enough to run away if it all goes south the first couple of times out.

Then, after the start-up equipment is in order, you're gonna need a target, so keep an eye out for areas in town that have big drug problems. You'll have to do some basic reconnaissance of the area in order to locate the local drug dealers; then you have to locate the flashiest, dumbest drug dealers, the ones with gold jewellery on display, fat wads of cash, and not a care in the world. If they deal hard drugs, that's the absolute best, for they'll pull in more business and are responsible for bigger societal problems. *These* guys are your ticket into the world of violent heroics; these guys are your start-up capital. Once you know who they are, learn their schedule, at least enough to know on what corner they deal at around 22:00 hours on Friday night...then you go and take their stuff at the 22nd hour on a convenient Friday (or Thursday, etc.).

Decide whether you're going to kill them or simply beat them into unconsciousness...possibly stun them with a Taser. Your initial instinct on this matter is vital; it is the indication of direction for your entire vigilante career. If you pick stunning or beating into unconsciousness, then you may want to steer towards street-level blunt force trauma style of crime-fighting, and avoid raiding meth labs with a shotgun. Anyway, whether he's dead or just incapacitated, take all his gold jewellery, along with his wallet. Now get the fuck out of there before anyone sees you! Evade detection at the scene, take whatever appearance altering steps are prudent, things of that nature; now go home.

Grab something to eat and congratulate yourself; you did good, and the first step to becoming super is to recognize your own greatness. ☺ As you enjoy your snack or feast, tally up the take; cash can be used right now, whereas gold, silver and jewels will be a source of additional Justice Funds along the way as the Crusade progresses.

Use that cash to buy the next thing(s) you need, and repeat when it becomes feasible...you will have to allocate time for each scene to cool down, and it would really be best to select new hunting grounds each time. This is your first step towards becoming a legend.

Once you have some of the things on your wish list, use some of that cash to establish yourself as an author. It's best if you can write, but if you can't, fret not, for there are ghostwriters to do the work if need be. The cheapest ones are in India, which has the largest English speaking population in the world; outsource your career and reap the benefit. Once you have a manuscript, use the cash to self-publish (and then pay for advertising afterwards), or to get an agent to aim at those traditional publishing houses. Either way, it costs a bit, but once it bears fruit, cool!

Depending on the level of literary success, one might be able to quit one's job entirely, or at least go to part-time status; it all depends on what serves your goals best. The ability to fly off to Pakistan and hunt Jihadi in the border regions might be your thing, or maybe buying a sweet tricked-out assault rifle is just the ticket. Perhaps what the extra cash buys is a 2-week, all-expenses paid luxury vacation for your wife and kids, so you can drive out west and blow up that parade of neo-Nazis with a gigantic bomb on a radio-controlled ATV...the point is that you now have options.

And with options comes freedom, the freedom to grow into your full hero potential, which leads to another level of crime-fighting exuberance. This next level also happens to be your next level of funding as well; raiding major drug houses and grow-ops. This may sound dangerous, but that's only because it is. Nothing worth having is zero risk, but being a superhero doesn't mean being a super-idiot; hence, armour the fuck up and get some kick-ass weapons going first. You'll probably want some of the goodies from a later chapter to take with you too, so spend quality time on preparations.

Once you have crossed into the realm of being able to take down relatively major organized crime nexus points, you will always have the necessary funds for whatever level of mission your burning compulsion to action desires. You'll also come across leads to other criminal operations to destroy, and will find various things to help in the ongoing battle which are just not available through legal channels; use the tools of crime to destroy itself, and gain extra hero points for ironic effect.

That's pretty much the basics of a tried-and-true method of financing a truly epic vigilante superhero career. As with most other parts of this book, you're encouraged to think outside the box, to look at things laterally rather than linearly. If you are an inventor rather than an author, use the funds to get that patent and development of concept under way. If you are the inheritor of a family fortune worth billions of dollars, forget everything I said about money, but perhaps still work through a progression of crime-fighting before tackling bigger international issues. However, if the inspiration hits you to hire a merciless band of mercenaries to help on your quest to destroy Somalian pirates, through the use of high-end weaponry produced by the manufacturing might of an old family friend who owed dear old dad a life-debt, hey, that works pretty damn well too.

But all this talk of drug lab/grow-op raids leads quite nicely into the next topic, because no matter how you feel about employing lethal force (I say go for it!), the opposition will have no qualms about firing indiscriminately in your direction. So let's go spit in the face of death, and find out some ways to keep from catching a nasty case of unsightly bullet holes. Quick, run for cover...but where?!?

{CHAPTER 12} "I'LL JUST HIDE BEHIND THAT BUSH...GACK!"...COVER VERSUS CONCEALMENT

We all know the drill: when the bullets fly it's time to get something between you and fast-flying chunks of lead. But not all objects are created equal, especially when it comes to their armour ratings. Just take a gander at this rather short scenario:

*As the gangsters pulled their rifles from the car's trunk, **Black Bolt** knew it was time to get behind the nearest available substantial object if he were to make it out alive. Luckily, a nearby SUV was easily accessible, so he ducked down beside it, using the doors to provide cover. The vicious thugs had seen him running that way, but he wasn't worried; let them waste their time and ammo while he came up with a plan to destroy them all.*

*The Russian mafia enforcers took aim at his hiding place, unleashing a torrent of .30 caliber death directly at the hero sheltered behind. The rifle rounds tore through the flimsy sheet metal and plastic with great ease, not slowed down to any appreciable degree. The bullet-ridden corpse of the **Black Bolt** sagged limply to the ground, and formed a sad pool of blood which would be his resting place till the undertakers arrived.*

So what went wrong? Why did the saga of the **Black Bolt** end in such a tragically lame sort of fashion? I mean, we see cops and crooks use cars as armoured firing points *all the time* in movies and on television; shouldn't the vehicle doors have done more to protect the stalwart defender of all that is good?

News flash: **television and movies are not real life.** They portray distortions of reality in a stylized fashion; dramatic effect, plot progression and looking cool are the main concerns, not factual accuracy. In addition, most of their writers don't know fuck-all about any of the things they are portraying, and most of their "fact" checking involves searching other fictional sources. This is not a problem as long as one remembers that entertainment is the goal, and therefore should not be used as a source for anything bearing the slightest resemblance to reality.

With that out of the way, let's get some solid reality underway. We'll start with simple definitions, **cover** and **concealment.** In the example above, the hero was seeking **cover;** cover is that which provides protection from bullets, shrapnel, and other nasty things that'll make you dead. What he actually found was **concealment,** that which hides you from the enemy; if they had not seen him run behind it, the SUV could have made decent concealment. There are of course options which offer both cover *and* concealment, which may be part of the problem for know-nothing Hollywood types doing the barest minimum of "research" for their projects. Here's a handy list of examples for you to get the point more thoroughly across:

- **Row of Hedges:** Concealment...hedges and bushes don't stop bullets.
- **Steel Dumpster:** This is an example of something which fulfills both functions; you can hide behind a dumpster, and most bullets won't be making it through. Hiding behind dumpsters is a good idea.
- **Cars and Trucks:** Unless it's a Brink's armoured truck, these are only good for concealment unless you can get right behind the wheels or engine block; those areas can actually provide some measure of protection. Just don't expect the doors of any production vehicle to stop bullets.
- **Dirt Berms:** Another great example of something which fulfills both functions, as long as the thickness of dirt is sufficient to the task (I'll show you the proper thickness shortly).
- **Trees:** Depending on the size of tree and the type of projectile, hiding behind a big tree can actually work for protection and concealment purposes. It'll generally have to be a pretty damn big tree though.
- **Interior walls:** Concealment only. Unless you're in a building designed to act as a bunker, those walls will be flimsy enough

to do nothing in the way of stopping bullets, even rather wimpy calibers. Use for hiding purposes only.

This small list should be enough to get you thinking along the right lines. Use your brain when on the go; thick concrete walls will provide protection against handgun rounds and most rifle rounds... but not all concrete is the same, so no guarantees. The big point here is to get the conceptual difference between the two, so that in the heat of the moment you pick the right choice; a pane of bullet-resistant glass would offer good ballistic protection, but it will make a really, really shitty hiding place to get the jump on crime from. Before we exit this section, I'll provide you with some handy data regarding the bullet resistance of various common materials. These are all values aimed at stopping various rifle rounds, so to stop handgun rounds the lowest thickness of material listed in each category should suffice.

- **Structural (mild) Steel:** Half an inch thick will stop 5.56mm or .30 caliber rifle rounds; three quarters of an inch thick will stop those as well as .50 caliber rifle/machinegun ammo.
- **Structural Aluminum:** One-inch-thick aluminum will stop 5.56mm and .30 caliber rifle rounds; two inches thick will stop those and .50 caliber as well.
- **Pine Wood:** Fourteen inches thick needed to stop 5.56mm; twenty-two inches to stop .30 caliber rounds; thirty-two inches of pine will stop those and .50 caliber rounds too.
- **Busted-up Stones (gravel/cobblestones/etc.):** Three inches stops 5.56mm; four inches stops .30 caliber; eleven inches stops .50 caliber death headed your way.
- **Wet Sand/Dirt:** Six inches to stop 5.56mm bullets; thirteen inches for .30 caliber; twenty-one inches required to stop .50 caliber.
- **Dry Sand:** Four inches for 5.56mm; five inches for .30 caliber; fourteen inches of dry sand will stop those nasty .50 caliber machinegun bullets from ruining your whole day.
- **Addendum:** These armour materials will wear away (ablate) under the repeated impacts from projectiles, and will need to be replenished in order to maintain armour effectiveness.

Obviously, most heroes aren't going to be in siege type situations, where fortification must be maintained to ensure overall ballistic protection and armoured firing points...although you might, who knows. It could also be helpful info in order to fortify one's home or base of operations in case of criminal or law enforcement raids, if the secret identity is compromised. The main point though is to give the superhero in the field all the tools needed to get the mission done, even when facing overwhelming odds.

Speaking of overwhelming odds, unless you simply stalk scum one at a time for silent removal from the Circle of Life, chances are you will often be outnumbered, sometimes by a fair bit. Thus, the next thing to look at is how one can deal with the issue of multiple opponents, armed or unarmed.

{CHAPTER 13} PHILOSOPHY OF FIGHTING MULTIPLE OPPONENTS

Fighting multiple opponents is always a challenge, but by approaching it with the correct attitude you'll be able to come out victorious. Besides, greater odds means greater glory, and your legend will grow by leaps and bounds once the bodies pile up, powerless against the sheer magnitude of your obvious greatness. So put all concerns for stupid things like being prudent aside as we examine what it takes to wage a successful one-man-versus-all war on evil.

Unarmed (or armed with small impact/blade weapons) Combat Against Multiple Unarmed Opponents:

All right, you're out there on the mean streets of the city late at night, but for some reason all the major weaponry got left at home. Maybe you set out for patrol just after work as an impromptu thing, or perhaps you just plain forgot the major gear. It could be that you're in a foreign land where the preferred items are just not available...it doesn't matter. What *does* matter is the gang of five jerks who decide they're going to invert the Justice equation by beating you into a bloody pulp; what do you do?

Well, there are a few schools of thought on this one, and they all have some merits depending on an assessment of the particular group being dealt with. The one most people are familiar with is the concept of *utterly destroying* the leader or biggest guy there, as an example to the rest that you are a threat they just cannot deal with. This one can indeed work, but there are some variables involved. First of all, you need to identify the leader; if the biggest guy isn't the "head wolf", so to speak, then destroying him may or may not do the trick. If the leader has actual authority over his underlings, he may still be able to get them roused to attack despite the destruction of one member, even the largest. Another consideration could be that one might need to go through their midst in order to get to the leader/big guy, which would invite attack on the way in. Remember, this isn't Westside Story, so the leader ain't necessarily going to come to the front and challenge you to a duel accompanied by rhythmic finger snapping by the rest of the gang.

This leads into the second idea, which is to simply destroy whoever is the closest as a demonstration of your deadly might. For either of these methods to work though, one thing is 100 percent necessary; you must *destroy the person in a spectacular fashion and with seeming ease*. **Example:** The first scum who gets within arm's reach gets his throat slashed wide open, showering those closest to him in a rain of blood**. Second example:** The first person who reaches you is the leader, and you knock him out with a single, glorious punch; alternately, you do a beautiful throw that sends him crashing to the pavement head first, with a squished skull leaking brains. The point is that the move has to be quick and efficient as well as totally devastating, so the rest of them feel there's no hope at all. Then they leave.

A third tactic is to run away, but not with the intent to outrun them all. The idea is that in any group one person will be quickest, which means he'll be the first person to catch up to you. What adds to your success is that you are only running to the first corner wall, or anything else which acts as an obstacle/visual disruptor, then stopping there till the fastest dude arrives. Then you kill/maim/knock him out...and start running again. This has the advantage of turning a five-on-one fight into a series of one-to-one fights; you also gain the blindsiding bonus whenever an effective obstacle is part of the equation. People have used this strategy to good effect in the past.

The fourth idea is based on controlling the angles of attack and having a keen sense of movement, yours and theirs. Basically it involves maneuvering so that only one person is being engaged at a time; by side-stepping, or stand-up grappling someone into the path of another at times, you can set it up so that you aren't being surrounded at any point. This requires good mobility and area awareness on your part, as well as the space required to do such a thing. As with the other methods, however, it requires the power or weaponry to make decisive, incapacitating damage with few movements at a time...if you get tangled up in a wrestling match, well, that's really going to suck for you.

Also, never discount the effectiveness of throwing people into each other; it is very effective and fun as hell too! This works best for high-level Hapkido and Aikido practitioners, as well as those heroes who are just really fucking strong. An inspirational real-life story involves an untrained engineer, of all things, who was the intended victim of a New York mugging by people with knives. He may not have known how to fight, but he sure was big...so he grabbed the nearest guy and threw him through a plate glass window! The rest of the muggers decided to get the hell out of there rather than face someone who was doing an effective impersonation of the Hulk. ☺

One more funny tidbit involves going unarmed against multiple opponents armed with medium sized knives. This one time I was up against two thugs armed with knives, so I maneuvered to the side of one (away from the hand with the blade) and shoved him onto the blade of his partner in crime! The resulting confusion and utter shock made it easy to get out of there. Moral of the story: keep calm and never doubt your own amazingness.

Armed with Large Impact or Blade Weapons Versus Others Similarly Armed:

Alright, when you're armed to this degree, you certainly have the ability to incapacitate the opponent with a single strike; unfortunately, they have the same power to direct back at you. Due to this fact, taking out the leader probably isn't as effective an option, unless the rest of the assholes don't really seem to have their hearts in it; if the lead dude is the one gung-ho to slice you up, killing him handily can make the others go away. You cannot operate under that assumption, however, so let's go look at strategies with a higher likelihood of lethal success.

Two of the strategies from the previous section work well here; controlling the line of attack, and the "run then kill the first guy to reach you" methodology. Controlling the line of attack is feasible, but far harder in this case due to their reach, and the nasty effect of their blows. So, although your mother told you to never run with scissors, I'm telling you to run with a baseball bat or short sword. One plus to the running method is that those pursuing you may fall on their own weapons...it happens sometimes. On that note, practice your running with weapons skills in advance, using training versions of whatever death-dealing devices are your personal favourite. That way one can avoid nasty self-inflicted wounds, plus gain a valuable edge on running speed versus the others, who likely will not have put that level of thought into things.

Of course, the absolute best way to deal with the situation in which a gang has you outnumbered and out-bladed is to pull out your trusty .357 Magnum revolver and shoot them in their stupid faces.

Armed with Firearms Versus Multiple Enemies Armed with Firearms:

Shots are ringing out all around. High-speed death fills the air and a single misstep could end your righteous Crusade in an instant...what do you do? Well, the first thing to do is get the fuck behind some effective cover, for the love of Odin! Don't stand out there like some moron from a bad action film, where all the scum are supplied with "bad guy bullets" incapable of harming the hero. This is real life with real consequences...

Let's rewind for a moment though, to a simpler time, before the lead started flying. With any luck and a bit of using one's brain, it should be possible to see such things coming before they reach that level, especially as *you're supposed to be the hunter,* not an unwitting target. Even the United States military forces get a feel for the area of deployment rather than just rushing in, and so should you. But whether things have been done properly or ended up with you hiding behind a dumpster or convenient pile of broken bricks and masonry, one thing remains the same; order of target engagement.

In general, you want to engage targets based on the threat level presented; a guy with an assault rifle or shotgun presents more threat than a thug wielding a .22 semi-auto pistol. If all threats seem equal as far as armament goes, engage those closest first, followed by the jerks further out afterwards. And if they're all behind a barricade themselves, it becomes a case of shoot whoever becomes visible first.

Threats can vary by other criteria than mere armament, however. The guy facing you is a more immediate threat than the dude looking away. That asshole further off may be next to a handy bit of cover, giving him the chance to be an ongoing threat if not taken out quickly enough. In general though, the closer they are with the more powerful weaponry, the bigger threat they pose. Just keep in mind the fact that all situations are fluid, especially those that involve multiple people; throwing guns into the mix just makes it even more so.

Bonus Section: "B" is for Bear Spray:

Not every crime merits death, and for those which don't, nothing does the trick quite like bear spray. It is effective, economical, and produces some fucking hilarious results. As an "area effect" weapon, it is also your best value for non-lethal Justice in group settings... check out this scenario:

You're hanging out in a major urban center, in the bar district at closing time. Mostly it's just the usual shambling, stumbling drunks, happily ambling along towards home to try and have sex before the effects of alcohol poisoning make it so their dicks don't work. Always good for a laugh, and maybe, if you're lucky, some hot chicks will flash their boobs at you...more often some dude will moon you instead; ick!

The crowds thin out, and the taxis become more infrequent, when hark! What's that sound? Is it, could it be...yes! The unmistakable sounds of assholes in combat call for your unique talents, so you make haste as fast as your feet (or bike/skateboard) can get you to the danger zone. A quick visual assessment of the scene shows 12 people engaged in lame, inefficient combat; poorly executed kicks; off-balance, drunken punches; a couple of people have knives drawn, but haven't managed better than a half-assed slash to a shoulder. They are definitely engaged in crime, but are really friggin inept; you must save them from themselves.

*Enter you, the heroic exemplar of Justice, armed with an aerosol can of salvation. Bursting into action, you depress the actuator, and a wide spray exits the nozzle, making it easy to rapidly fill the entire combat zone with a burning chemical fog. Everyone starts choking, gagging, coughing and reaching towards blurry, useless eyes. Since your eyes are protected by goggles it has no effect on you (you **are** wearing your protective goggles, right?), allowing for an easy escape from the chaos with no consequences at all...just get the fuck out of there, okay?*

The day is saved; in the aftermath of a glorious cloud of bear spray, none of those fuckers is thinking about continuing to fight each other <u>at all</u>. Seriously, they'll barely remember their own names right then, let alone anything else at all...except that they really hate whoever sprayed them, which is why you got the fuck out of Dodge and headed to Tim Horton's for a well-deserved donut or three.

Yep, a can of bear spray can make the enterprise of pacifying the streets far more manageable; no crime-fighting superhero vigilante should leave home without it. And although the above example is of a non-lethal intervention, it is just as valuable in more brutal applications as well. Just imagine the advantage you'll have when your enemies cannot see properly and are struggling for breath. Pair a knife, sword or baseball bat with bear spray, and you have a truly winning combination.

Other pepper spray products can certainly be used as well, but even the huge honkin cans that law enforcement use for crowd/riot control are designed to come out in a stream which can be aimed. In certain situations, this is preferable (so keep that in mind), but for crowd control effectiveness by a single person, I recommend you go with the fogging action of bear spray. That fogging action is also great for those rare situations when you need to bravely run away; just spray behind as you flee, and any pursuers will have a very difficult time following...unless they have gas masks (but that's what caltrops are for... ☺).

Now you're armed with the info needed to tackle those larger groups when out there on the mean streets battling crime on your own. There's something inherently satisfying about being able to take on the world with no back-up, a one-man wrecking ball aimed at the dark heart of criminal scum across the land. The section just concluded may get you thinking on a different track, however; if criminals can group together, why not heroes? And yes, this approach is seen in the mundane world, where police and militaries form into organizations devoted to combating evil—as they see it, at any rate—so the idea is not entirely without merit.

It is also not without pitfalls and risks though, especially when one is operating outside the protective aegis of societally sanctioned authority. Thus, we shall next examine it all—the good, the bad, and the merely annoying—as I peel back the aura of mystique surrounding that other mainstay of heroic literature, the **super-team.**

{CHAPTER 14} SUPER-TEAMS: ASSET OR LIABILITY?

You could try the "theme based" approach: here we see the all-female super-team, fully accessorized and deadly. Sadly, the third member of the team caught a nasty case of death whilst battling a villain, and couldn't appear in this photo.

There's no doubt that having back-up in a fire-fight can be a good thing; likewise, no one will argue that having five buddies with them didn't help during that bar-room brawl. In the realm of military or police actions, sure there are snipers or the lone patrol cop, but when the shit hits the fan they send in the Marines or SWAT. So I guess you should immediately start recruiting prospective superheroes down at the martial arts school and gym locker room, right?

Not so fast...there's a reason that snipers and beat cops still exist; not every goal requires or benefits from a team approach, for one thing. If the Marines charge into action, the commotion can give the enemy leader advance warning enough to escape the reach of Justice...but a sniper can take him out before the alarm can be raised. SWAT doesn't stand a chance of infiltrating a drug operation, but a lone undercover guy can do what those heavily armed and armoured dudes cannot. However, even these rather apt examples act as a roundabout endorsement of the team approach, as they have back-up; they are not lone vigilantes.

So what should you decide on, and based on what criteria? That's a good question, and although I know the answer suited to my own crime-fighting efforts, your requirements and goals may need a different approach. In order to get at the heart of your personal truth, we'll examine some pros and cons to each approach—solo or team—building a database that you can use to make an appropriate decision. Let's go!

Having Back-up: This is an undisputable benefit to the team approach, and is one the main reasons anyone goes that route in the first place. Whether storming a major crack-house SWAT-style or sending one team member to do the whole mission while the team stands by for extraction, having those extra people around adds a layer of safety lacking in the lone wolf approach.

Type and Scale of Operations Possible: No matter how mighty and heroic you may rise to become, you are still limited by reality to occupying a single point in space-time. Ergo, you cannot be in 2, 3, or 7 places simultaneously...but 2, 3, or 7 people can. Think of the A-Team, where one guy is setting off a bomb, another guy is disabling locking mechanisms, while yet another sneaks in to free the captives. This is the sort of thing possible when numbers are on your side; you can hit multiple positions at the same time. Being able to simultaneously multi-task also adds to mission types as well as scale, for while a single hero could indeed destroy a small military outpost—using methods I'll show you in another chapter—he could not so easily free hostages from such a situation.

Camaraderie: This is the other big driving force in the creation of super-teams (or teams of any sort, for that matter). As social creatures, humans feel a need for belonging, as well as the sense that others understand them. They need people who will listen to their trials and tribulations, then nod in that particular way which says "Yep, been there before." Crime-fighting superheroes aren't likely to find such understanding from friends not involved with such things, nor are their spouses going to offer the proper support or advice (with very few exceptions). Seeing as this is a facet of the human condition, few heroes will be *super* enough to bear up under the pressures attendant to the enterprise on their own; for them, the support network of fellow crime-fighters will be vital to maintaining good mental health.

The dynamic duo is another popular variant;
many of the benefits, while limiting the liability.

Brain-storming Ideas: "Two heads are better than one" is the old folk wisdom, and indeed this often proves to be the case. The atomic bomb—one of the most potent evil eliminating devices yet devised—would never have come to fruition if not for a massive team effort. Likewise, battle-plans for all the greatest conquests throughout history have had input from others, even if one man was the chief architect. By forming a like-minded group of heroes dedicated to the cause of Justice, you can harness this power for yourself as well. While one person may come up with what seems to be a great plan of action, his fellow comrade may see a glaring flaw, simply by looking at things from a different perspective. We all have different backgrounds, and therefore bring varying points of view to the table. **Cons:** *We all have differing backgrounds and bring varying points of view to the table.* The very thing which can be a mighty strength also has potential to be a debilitating flaw. For every plan that bears fruit from brain-storming success, another group ends up in bitter deadlock, endlessly bickering over minutiae.

Cons of the Team Approach/Strengths of Going it Solo:

Freedom of Action: Due to the collaboration inherent to the team approach, individual freedom of choice and action will be limited. Since the actions of one can affect the success of all, you'll not be free to follow any whim which pops into your head. Those who insist on exercising what they see as their right to act independently usually end up booted from the team. Going it solo, therefore, allows for complete freedom of expression; follow your thirst for Justice wherever it may lead!

Going it solo can look really fucking awesome sometimes. Lurking up above, ready to pounce...it can be pretty great.

Potential for Betrayal: Let's face it; you cannot afford to have the world at large learn your secret identity. If they knew about your heroic actions, rather than awarding a medal they'd chuck you in prison for all eternity. If the criminals found out, well, it could go really badly for friends and family. At the very least it would require a complete restructuring of one's life; new identity; new place to live...pain in the ass.

Another old saying is "Loose lips sink ships", and the more lips there are, the greater chance of things slipping out. All it takes is one moronic moment of indiscretion by a single member of the team for the rest of you to be fighting for mere survival. This constitutes the greatest weakness of a team approach to what must be a clandestine endeavour; it is also another strength of the solo vigilante option. As long as you can keep your own fool mouth shut, the secret remains safe.

That pretty much sums up the main points for or against forming a super-team. Every hero must decide if the risks outweigh the benefits, especially when the stakes are so high. I will mention that due to what all is at stake, most people prefer to go the solo route, entrusting their deepest thoughts to a diary if need be as an emotional outlet (just make sure that if you do so, it remains safely hidden; it would make a prosecutor's job stupid easy).

But whether you decide on a team approach or choose to go it alone, at some point you'll run across scum vile enough to merit a lengthier, more individualized form of punishment. Even if this never becomes an issue due to a preference for instant scum removal versus the drawn-out alternatives, eventually the need for critical information will arise, along with the requirement for "Enhanced interrogation techniques." Although torture on-the-go yields some useful results, your brutal reign of Justice will benefit greatly from a sound-proofed and well-stocked dedicated *Lair of Death*.

{CHAPTER 15} BUILDING YOUR VERY OWN LAIR OF DEATH

Having a functional __Lair of Death__ will really increase your Justice options.

Before I get down to the subject matter at hand, I need to address a few things. Most of the civilized world eschews torture—at least officially—so it's little surprise that discussion of the topic brings out such heated emotions. But before you get all huffy and start screaming about how "Torture is wrong! It has no uses for anything ever! No exceptions!!!" just sit back and consider the following scenario:

A lone figure stalks through the darkness of an abandoned warehouse; this part of town hasn't been used for any productive purpose in years, and now it festers like an open wound. The police generally avoid patrolling around here, and the private security companies contracted for insurance purposes pay their guards so little that it isn't worth the hassle for them to do any interior patrols ever. This has led to the state of affairs which sees a solitary hero seeking degenerate scum within its depths.

From ahead and just around a corner come the sound of muffled sobs; the object of tonight's hunt is near. The vigilante sneaks silently forward...the prey must be given no opportunity to escape the hand of Justice. He reaches the corner and stealthily peers around; he gags at the sight now in view, repulsive beyond anything he has ever witnessed in the past.

A 10-year-old girl is strapped over a chair, screaming in pain as the disgusting animal tortures her with a knife. She is covered in cuts, many of them scabbed over or held together with crude stiches; he has been at this for days, weeks even perhaps. Not only that, but body parts of other children hang from hooks at the end of chains, creating the abattoir atmosphere this perverted freak revels in.

With a cry of disgust and rage, the hero rushes forward at full tilt, unable to restrain himself. With gloved hands he punches the slime-bucket to the ground, continuing till his knuckles get raw despite the leather covering them. Pulling his stun-gun he zaps the bastard till the batteries run dry, then secures him hand and foot with a generous amount of duct tape. Chest heaving with exertion, tears of rage welling in the corners of his eyes, he surveys the scene, trying to come up with a plan.

Finally, he figures it out, and resolutely the plan is implemented. The van gets backed-up to the nearest door, and the asshole is shoved in the back, covered with a sheet after his mouth is taped shut. As he drives off, a call gets placed to 9-1-1 so emergency personnel can provide the medical care the poor girl so desperately needs (the call is made from a cheap throw-away cellphone). With grim determination the vigilante mentally prepares himself for what must follow...death is too good for this type of scum, or at least a quick death is.

What say you now? I'll bet the disgust rose in an unstoppable wave as you read what was happening, only to change into burning rage against all who would dare to do such abominable things. No punishment is too much for such degenerate slime, no matter how long and drawn out it may be. To kill him instantly would help balance things out to a certain extent, as he'd be removed from the equation...but removal is not the same as balancing. In order to balance the Justice equation fully he must be made to suffer an equal quantity of pain, degradation and fear. The specifics may indeed be of a differing nature—for to do the exact things some of these perverts commit would lower one to their level of filth—but the level of suffering must be equaled. This takes time, creativity and privacy, things which require a specific setting. Your very own *Lair of Death* will provide the time, privacy and tools necessary to get truly medieval on those retrograde fucks.

But even if such things are just too brutal for your sensibilities (which is okay; we need all types of heroes in this fight ☺), there are those situations where vital information may require extraction from those unwillingly to bend under normal pressure. The classic example is the villain who has placed a bomb in a school/hospital/nursing home or something of that manner, and it is set to explode soon. You cannot evacuate until you know where it actually is...thousands of lives are at stake...time is of the essence...*what do you do?* Will you let thousands of innocent lives be ended just because of squeamishness? Or will you hero-up, grab the blowtorch and get that location **now?**

Or maybe you need a personal motivation; what if the life of your wife, husband, daughter or son were on the line? Would you let your father be eaten by a tank full of moray eels—him dangling over it with a time-release mechanism—or would you grab a potato peeler and start removing skin till the requisite answers were at hand?

Well, if you'd let your own father get eaten by eels to save the skin of an evil villain, then **fuck you, you absolute piece of shit!** Stop reading this book and go jump in a wood-chipper feet first (man, what kind of fucking low-life would let their own dad get eaten by eels...)

For everyone else with the moral integrity and intestinal fortitude needed to get the job done, join me as we examine what you need to know in order to set up a truly horrifying (and effective) interrogation/torture chamber...your very own *Lair of Death*.

Location, Location, Location:

We all know that in the game of selling real estate location is a huge factor in desirability and asking price; some locations offer better access to schools, shopping, or perks such as beautiful scenery for relaxing walks through velvety forests. When it comes to deciding upon where to locate your dungeon, location is still a key factor, but the specific things being looked for will of course be slightly different.

As a brutal superhero, you have a lot to balance; your civilian and crime-fighting identities must remain separate; family demands might need to be met...it's quite a challenge. If you haven't fully divorced yourself from the demands of work using my proven methods—which I'll again recommend—then your working life somehow has to be fit into the mix as well! Between work, family, exercise and occasional sleep, crime-fighting activities are hard enough to schedule; hence, travel time to your *Lair of Death* becomes a factor. This may lead one towards locating it at home...but there are also drawbacks to be considered.

Home-Sweet-Home: By building it into your residence, travel time can be kept to a minimum. Criminals can be tortured for a couple of hours in the morning and you still end up making that early morning meeting at work on time. If travel time to and from the interrogation area were the only concern, this would seem a no-brainer; however, there are many other considerations as well.

If you live with a spouse and kids, how will you sneak bad guys past them, and how do you sneak the mangled corpses out? Won't nosey neighbours be likely to see that squirming sack you're lugging into the house or shed out back? And if you live in an apartment, forget it; not enough space and way too many witnesses all around. Even if you're lucky enough to live on a property with ample space for a properly sound-proofed, spacious shed with strong walls and secure locks, no neighbours for half a mile in every direction...how will you explain to your wife why she's never, **never** to go in there? Disregard that issue if your wife has joined you on the path of harsh Justice; the couple who slays together stays together.

Unless you live on a decent sized piece of land out in the country by yourself, the at-home approach is probably not a great choice. The only other time such a thing could work would be a bachelor in the city who lives in a house with an attached garage and a door leading straight inside from it; with additional sound proofing and a few other upgrades it becomes feasible. In those circumstances then yes, it becomes an option...but it requires maintaining the living single lifestyle (unless your life-mate is also a violent vigilante), and this may not be an attractive option for many folks.

Urban-Decay Zone: If you're lucky enough to live in a major urban center that has experienced significant decay, this option could be right for you! Not only are you lucky enough to live in an area where violent criminals are easily accessible, but opportunities abound for a *Lair of Death* with great natural ambience as well. I'm talking about all those wonderful abandoned warehouses, factories and boarded up houses; crime makes good use of them, and so should you.

As a great example, up near Toronto a number of years back there was a major grow-op located in an old abandoned brewery. We're talking about a *major* operation too, practically industrial in scale... yet it operated sight unseen for years. Think about all the materials which had to go in, along with all the personnel going in and out, along with illegal electricity drainage (which is how they finally found out about it...dumbasses should have bought a generator or some shit like that; solar panels even). A small torture operation could operate for years in such a location.

If one is lucky enough to live in a decrepit hole like Detroit, well that's just perfect! With a little soundproofing material and padlocks you can transform an abandoned house or back-office of an abandoned factory into a dandy little dungeon; equipped with an alarm system that alerts you to any breach of security, you'll reap the benefits of an off-site location, while still remaining many steps ahead of getting caught. And in a great place like Detroit, the options are almost endless due to decades of decay and financial meltdown. A city built for 1.5 million people now has only half that population, so you have literally a city's worth of places to repurpose to brutal ends. And travel time is still kept to a minimum as long as your urban-decay house of pain is in your city of residence. This makes a grand choice for many gritty, hard-edged vigilantes.

Remote Mountain or Woods Hideaway: A purpose-built cabin out in the woods in a remote mountain fastness offers the ultimate in seclusion, providing maximum privacy for punishing evildoers and wringing the secrets out of diabolical malcontents. If in Canada or certain sections of the United States, vast swathes of undisturbed land can be found, where no one will hear the screams (they shouldn't anyway though...soundproofing, remember?). As an added bonus, it'll give you a chance to reconnect with nature, exploring the untamed wilderness and breathing in the clean, unpolluted air.

There is of course the matter of roads...how will you get to your mountain fastness without them? Well, you could blaze trails and use an ATV to get your prisoners there, but it might be a better idea to buy some land (Northern Ontario has big tracts of land for dirt cheap prices; same goes for some less populated US states), and then build upon it. Your *Lair of Death* will look much like a tool shed when unoccupied anyway, so as long as a nice little cabin is built to accompany it, it will all look perfectly normal. Hell, you can take the wife for a romantic getaway and enjoy some hot cabin sex when the *Tool Shed of Justice* isn't being used.

The downside of it all is massive travel time; quite simply put, you'll have a hard time getting the evil jerk there in time to ferret out the bomb location in time to save all those kids/virgins/whales/whatever. For punishment purposes when time is not of the essence, however, one would be hard pressed to find a better option.

Proper Construction:

Whichever option you do choose to go with, certain essentials must be addressed. The first and foremost of these is soundproofing; even if you keep the prisoner gagged for most of it, they'll scream bloody murder as soon as it's removed for questioning. Even if your neighbours are selfish, uncaring jerks who wouldn't lift a finger to save a drowning child, they'll still call the cops to make a noise complaint, which will make for an awkward conversation at the very least. Even in your mountain retreat, if that's the option gone with, you will run the risk of hikers innocently blundering by...why take the chance that someone will hear and think they're doing the right thing by summoning the police? A smart hero leaves nothing to chance.

You're also going to need a way to keep weaselly scum from squirming free of their well-deserved torment. For this purpose, a sturdy steel chair bolted to the ground is best; get one with solid steel armrests so you can handcuff/chain them to it. If anchoring things to cement floors isn't your bag, then a good alternative is a heavy steel table with slots suitable for securing chains or other restraints. The steel table option also allows for use in construction projects, and won't look incriminating in the same way as a bolted-down chair might. If you go with the urban-decay dungeon setting, chances are that a suitably heavy and immobile object will already be on hand to serve in this capacity.

Pegboard is great for all your tool holding needs; simply arrange the hooks in a suitable fashion, and there you go! Not only is this method convenient, it also adds that utilitarian look which is so important if people are ever going to see it in a casual setting. Those operating out of an abandoned warehouse or factory may prefer to simply bring a toolbox containing the requisite implements rather than leaving them there; they'll also likely find abandoned tools on site which can do a pretty good job on their own. ☺

Last but not least is the need for sturdy doors and locks. You don't need your prisoner getting away if he somehow squirms away as a restraint is being applied or loosened (before you can tackle him, that is), nor do you really want uninvited visitors coming in while an interrogation is in progress, or while you're away. Sturdy padlocks can easily be installed in abandoned factories, and they generally already have sturdy doors in key areas.

Tools of the Trade:

Simple tools readily found around the house can really put the hurt on crime in a big, big way.

As with any endeavour in life, the proper tools will ensure that success comes far more easily. Luckily, many of the essential tools are used for more mundane tasks, and will therefore not arouse suspicion by their mere possession. In fact, many of them will likely be in your tool kit already...although you may want extras anyway (they'll get all kinds of gross from use).

Hammers: You're going to want a wide assortment of hammers. Sledgehammers are great for crushing large bones, but smaller ones will allow for targeting specific anatomical bits. Rawhide or rubber mallets are handy when you want to inflict more bruising type of damage as opposed to outright destruction of body parts. Don't discount the amazingly aggravating effects of applying a small brass hammer to various areas either...psychological distress may serve your purposes better at times, so cover all bases.

Pliers: A mainstay of obtaining information throughout the ages, pliers can be used effectively by just about anyone regardless of prior experience. Grab some part of the body and pull, twist or crush; it's that easy. Try heating them with a blowtorch first for variety.

Blowtorches: At some point a blowtorch is going to come in handy. They're useful for all sorts of things, including heating metal implements for burning, branding, or even cauterizing wounds to prevent excessive blood loss. Application of the flame itself is pretty self-explanatory.

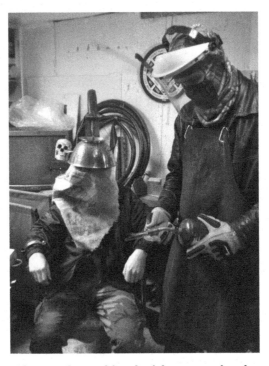

Blowtorch combined with a saw: simple,
yet effective! (Yes, I did find out where
the bomb had been planted... ☺)

Pellet/BB Guns: Not many people think of pellet guns for such uses, but they offer a great way to inflict non-lethal shooting damage during the interrogation/punishment process. Whether you choose pneumatic pump-up, spring powered or CO_2 versions, these readily available items can work wonders. Shoot that child molester a few times in the testicles and just watch his attitude change right before your eyes!

Vices: Useful for slow, steady application of crushing pressure to any body part which fits within their jaws. I'll leave the rest to your imagination.

Assorted Others: Nails, staples, saws, power sanders, utility knives, battery acid...you should be getting the basic concept by now. The point is that with time, privacy and grim determination, no level of scum is beyond being broken, regardless of how tough they start off believing themselves to be.

This concludes what was of necessity a rather dark and disturbing section. In fact, if you weren't at least a tad disturbed I'd be awfully worried about the state of your sanity. However, truly evil monsters exist out there in the real world, and they are far more disturbing in their capacity to do harm than anything contained herein. Building off of that, undoubtedly your vigorous efforts in the *Lair of Death* will yield leads on some really juicy targets, the sort of evil most men cannot even imagine in their worst nightmares. Eliminating degenerate scum operating at this level may require tools beyond knives, clubs and guns...well fear not, brave soul, for the next few chapters will provide you with the requisite tools needed to prevail.

{CHAPTER 16} WEAPONS OF MASS AWESOMENESS: HOMEMADE INCENDIARIES AND EXPLOSIVES

"You can't hug your children with nuclear arms" was the old hippy chant, and indeed it is true. However, Dresden (fire-bombing) and Hiroshima (nuclear annihilation) showed the effectiveness of overwhelming force applied against stubborn, potent enemies. Nuclear arms are the pure force of retribution distilled.

You won't have access to that level of destructive force, but you can apply the same principles. Take your own brutal Crusade against evil to new heights by adding the power of explosives and the fiery fury of incendiaries. By learning to craft effective destructive devices by one's own artifice, you will never be found wanting when taking the fight to truly heinous and organized threats. So let's get this party started with a bang!

Gunpowder:

Although it's one of the first effective explosives mankind ever developed, good old-fashioned gunpowder remains just as useful to the rampaging superhero of today as it was hundreds of years ago. Whether you live in an oppressive country and need it to power home-made firearms, or just need something to wipe out a huge crowd of neo-Nazi scum, black powder will satisfy your Justice requirements very well.

Whether Roger Bacon, Berthold Schwarz, or some anonymous Chinese alchemist whose name is lost to the ages was the person to first stumble upon the correct mixture is entirely irrelevant. What is relevant though is the proper mixture of the correct ingredients. For the original bad boy of demolition, the chemical composition is: **75% saltpeter; 15% charcoal; 10% sulfur. Amounts are determined by weight.**

There is a slight bit more than just mixing it up and lighting a match, however; that will work (sort of), but the mixture separates during transport, making a really shitty and unreliable propellant/explosive. So you have to wet it (really, really wet it) with alcohol or water, and form it into "cakes" of black powder which are then broken into smaller chunks by hand, then mortar and pestle, to be finally passed through various sizes of screen to refine powder size. The process could look like this: *pour powder ingredients into metal pan; stir with wooden spoon...add enough water to make a slurry. Some people like to heat the mixture but not to a boil (duh!). Have a bucket of alcohol sitting handy: pour the slurry into the bucket of alcohol. Let it sit for a while, then strain out the powder by passing the alcohol/black powder mix through cheesecloth. Squeeze out all moisture, forming a lump o' explosive. Let it dry, break it into smaller bits and voila!*

Caution: The basic recipe for black powder is <u>not a secret</u>: this means other people will quite likely know what the fuck you're up to if they see all the components being amassed at once. So don't go down to your local drug store and ask for their entire supply of saltpeter and sulphur...be smart about it. Buy small bits from different stores; get some from chemical supply houses, one ingredient at a time. The one exception, naturally, is charcoal due to the fact that it gets used for barbequing. Don't buy briquettes though; that shit ain't all charcoal.

<u>Canadian Proviso</u>: Due to the government's inclusion of United Nation's *Pussy Regulation number 1486* into Canada's *Explosives Act*, you can no longer get saltpeter at the local drug store. You CAN buy it from chemical supply houses for a higher price...you must, however, provide government issued photo identification <u>and</u> the reason you want it. For Canadian crime-fighters, it is easier to simply go your local gun-store and **buy the finished product**, which, for some reason, doesn't require a firearms license (at this point...governments love making laws, so who knows what it'll be like next week).

Napalm:

This is a truly nasty thing, developed for use in the crucible of war. It is basically jellied gasoline, meaning it sticks onto whatever it's throw/stuck/blown onto; once set on fire, look out! It's hard to get off and burns at very hot temperatures. Used extensively in the Vietnam War, it got a bad name due to bad publicity. We're enthusiastically violent superheroes though, we don't give a damn about things like that; certainly if evil can be effectively burned to a crisp by utilizing it and oh baby, it sure can. ☺

One of the greatest things about it is how amazingly simple it is to make effective versions of it with common household items that won't raise eyebrows. There are **two very simple** recipes I'll be sharing with you; and all you need is gasoline, Styrofoam cups, and Ivory brand bar soap. Oh yeah, and a wooden stick will come in handy. Who could believe that something so effective could be so simple to make, eh?

Recipe #1: Pour gasoline into a bucket or other container. Break up Styrofoam cups (or insulation) into little pieces, and place them into the gasoline while you stir it with a wooden stick. Keep adding Styrofoam while stirring until the desired level of "goopiness" is achieved. *That's it!*

Recipe #2: Shred some Ivory brand bar soap with a cheese grater; place the shredded soap out in the sun for a while to make sure it's good and dry. Then put some gasoline in a metal bucket; add shredded soap while stirring with a wooden stick until desired consistency is achieved. Some people like to heat the gasoline with a hot-plate to facilitate dissolving of the soap...your choice, just don't burn yourself to death. *That's it!*

Thermite:

Okay, this one's going to take a little more scrounging on your part... scratch that, it turns out to be really fucking easy finding what you need on the internet. One of the first search engine results came back with a supplier that sells every single ingredient you need for the military grade thermite! How goddamned cool is that? The internet, making everything easier, even superheroics. Beware, crime, the Digital Age has become your downfall.

Thermite: Mix **76.3%** iron oxide (rust) with **23.7%** aluminum powder. Mix by weight. This is pretty close to an 8:3 ratio by weight.

Military Grade Thermite: Simply mix **68.7%** thermite with **2%** sulfur, **29%** barium nitrate, and stir in some water with **0.3%** dextrin (dextrin is a water soluble binder used commonly in pyrotechnics). You can use corn starch if dextrin isn't available. Let the mixture dry and you're good to go. Magnesium strips/powder can be used as an ignition source, although I'll show you a more fun alternative for Justice-on-the-go in a little bit.

Uses: Handy uses include any time you need to burn through metal, so why not burn through stubborn locks or chains that obstruct the path to vengeance? Captured criminals will likely spill their secrets when thermite is burning through their femur, so as an information gathering device it has potential. Or simply set a heap of it ablaze on top of a metal roof of a building containing a gathering of criminal minds...watch the hilarity ensue as burning metal falls upon their stupid evil heads.

Molotov Cocktails:

The humble Molotov cocktail has been the bane of mechanized troops fighting against under-armed resistance fighters for generations. Ever since 1939 it has been a great way to even the odds, splashing your enemies in a burning film of retribution (and gasoline). Simple and quick to make out of commonly found materials, it can be a handy tool in your repertoire as well. If it can take out tanks when used correctly, just think what it can do for you!

Basic Recipe: Simply take a glass bottle, fill it with gasoline (but not all the way to the top...you do have to throw it!), then stick a rag in the neck of the bottle, but not far enough that it reaches into the fluid. The wick can be soaked in kerosene or diesel to make it burn well enough for the purpose. You could just use gasoline for it too, but it's not quite as good. When the glass bottle hits what you throw it at, the wick sets the gasoline on fire for a hefty dose of burning Justice!

Considerations: If you use flimsier glass you can have it burst when hitting targets that aren't quite as hard, or if the throw isn't the best. Oil can be added to the mixture to change the burning properties... and apparently Molotov cocktails containing home-made napalm have been used to good effect. Which brings up the next idea.

Mega-Molotov Cocktail: If you add thermite to napalm, it will ignite during the burning process. So why not mix some thermite into that napalm, and then use it to make your Molotov cocktail? Leave enough room above the napalm for some fluid gasoline to help ensure nice ignition when the bottle breaks. Adding burning power on top of burning power = awesome. Remember to always exercise your creativity and lateral thinking skills in this wondrous adventure; you'll have more success and fun than if you get trapped into strictly following the rules.

Bombs (I am the Midnight Bomber That Bombs at Midnight...)

Bombs have gotten a bad rap over the years due to indiscriminate use by terrorists, morons, and armies behaving like moronic terrorists. This is the fault of the humans using them though, not the devices themselves! A bomb which vapourizes NAMBLA, removing those boy-fucking scum from the face of the planet, is a good thing. Likewise, no one can dispute the benefits of hurling a hefty pipe bomb into a room full of meth-dealing rapists before entering oneself to execute those still living. For those who like mundane examples, those scenic mountain passes you like driving along wouldn't be passable if not for the explosives—bombs—that blasted the extra rock out of the way. In the correct hands, bombs are a force for good.

Since yours are obviously among the correct hands, let's learn the basics of making some kick-ass explosive devices. First, some

115

theory: when a propellant like gunpowder is ignited, it produces a bunch of hot, rapidly expanding gases. If you contain those gases, pressure builds in double-quick time. If the containment vessel is not strong enough, an explosion occurs as the gases violently blast it apart. Damage can be caused by the shockwave itself, as well as by shrapnel from the container. Extra shrapnel can be provided to increase damage; this is indeed a feature of many bombs aimed at causing mass body damage, injuries and death.

Pipe Bombs: The container is either a plastic or metal pipe (copper or steel often) filled with gunpowder, capped at both ends with a fuse of some sort to ignite it. The choice of metal or plastic pipe—and size of the bomb—will depend on its intended purpose. If you're making a flash-bang to cause disorientation when you storm a room, something smaller made with a thinner plastic pipe would be a good choice. If you're trying to destroy all the people in the room, then a far larger bomb made with metal pipe would be a better choice.

Whatever your choice, make sure to pack the pipe tightly; tamp that gunpowder down. Whether you're using a fuse coming through the side-wall of the pipe or an end cap, place the fuse before packing in the powder. Seal the fuse hole with some hot glue to ensure a nice tight fit. Cannon fuse is a common choice for people making bombs of this size, which are intended for throwing. Remote detonation bombs will use electrical ignition, and model rocket igniters are rather often the choice then.

Make sure the end-caps are really, really tightly secured, or you'll make more of a shitty gun than a bomb, as the end flies off into the distance. On plastic ones I've seen hot glue and lots of duct tape used; for metal pipes choose ones with threaded ends. Crimped and folded ends could be used as well on copper, but probably best to stick with threaded steel pipe instead.

Shrapnel Bombs: Start with a basic pipe bomb design at the center of it, and surround it with a larger container/pipe which is filled with ball bearings, nails, lead balls/bullets, or anything else which seems to be nasty. If you want to get more shrapnel-tastic, use a rotary tool or files to create a pattern of horizontal and vertical lines forming little squares, just like on those fragmentation grenades so often seen deactivated at gun shows. Then the casing should blast apart into shrapnel as well, if you're lucky. Don't forget, you're gonna need a tube going through the outer casing into the inner casing to provide an ignition channel; that small tube gets filled with powder and a fuse prior to *go time.*

You can also try filling the outer casing (the bigger pipe) with napalm as well; it certainly won't make the results any more pleasant for the targets, and come on, flaming bad guys! Give it a try and see what the ancient gods of retribution decide to grace you with.

I think that's probably enough information to get you soundly started on the path of burning and blasting a bloody path through the criminal underworld. It will certainly provide the means to up the ante as regards operation size; even a simple pipe bomb will aid immensely in raiding major drug houses. In order to rack up a truly legendary body count, however, you're going to need a means of delivering massive payloads to the target area; I'm talking about devices even Beast from X-Men couldn't lift, in some cases. To really ramp it up you're going to need something else...but fear not, for it's coming right up; your very own bomb delivery vehicle.

{CHAPTER 17} JUSTICE COMES FROM OVER THE HILL: BOMB DELIVERY VEHICLES

You've been practicing your skills; gunpowder is no problem to manufacture, and that new, proprietary blend of napalm tested yesterday took an hour to fully extinguish. Perhaps a few crack-houses around town have "mysteriously" exploded...what more could you need at this point, right? Let me paint you a picture of the future; just put down the Molotov cocktail and relax for a minute:

It's a beautifully sunny day in mid-July, not a cloud in sight and the humidity is just right for a change. Birds are singing, and new love is being discovered by young and old as they venture out into the majesty which is God's creation. Not much more could be asked for by anyone, and at times like this it's easy to believe that all is right with the world, and humanity is on an upward swing into a glorious new future of peace and prosperity. Or at least it is if you stay in this park...

Across the province the weather is the same, but a different mood is in the air. The atmosphere is one of bigotry, stupidity and abject hatred. Today is the gathering of Aryan Pride Canada, and they aren't singing songs of peace and love. The schedule is strictly regimented for this event, complete with workshops on "racial theory", "defending racial purity", and other more physical skills. Small arms practice is being done off to the side; small unit tactics are practiced with paintball markers; how to extract poisons from various plants is yet another thing being taught, complete with practical, hands-on instruction. Swastikas and Nazi salutes are the order of the day...the future begins to look less bright.

When hark, what crests the hill and rolls down the winding road into the semi-hidden woodland hate-camp area? It appears to be a cargo van, rather nondescript and slightly dented; nothing too odd. Except... wasn't everyone invited to this Hitler-fest already present? What gives?

Wary eyes watch the vehicle's approach, and combat shotguns are brought to the ready position; if this jerk wants a fight he'll have one! But wait...that's odd...where is the driver...is that a camera...?

Two miles away a man sits in a comfortable chair, manipulating a remote controller mounted beside an LCD display screen showing a view of Nazi-wannabe scum toting shotguns. He smiles, then flips up the cover over a red button; the button is pressed. A radio signal is sent through the airwaves, igniting a small electric model rocket igniter in the rear of a van over yonder.

"BOOOOOM!!!" *is the sound of Justice roaring through the countryside. The video screen has gone to black, but that's only natural seeing as what was in the rear of the van. 300 pounds of black powder in a heavy-duty steel casing weighing hundreds of pounds. Barrels of napalm enhanced with thermite arranged around the explosive device, a sprinkling of nails for extra shrapnel joy; extra jugs of a gasoline/oil mix added carefully till the weight limit of the vehicle was almost exceeded. Now, all that remains is twisted metal, billowing black smoke, and burning, broken bodies.*

As the sound dissipates in its onward travel to announce the return of sanity to a sometimes divided land, a strange peace settles in. The anonymous hero stands and stretches, limbering up after sitting in concentration so intently. He whistles a jaunty, uplifting tune, and puts the chair back into the car. The GPS provides the shortest route to his favourite restaurant in the area, a seafood and steak joint. Mmmmm yes, a lobster would certainly hit the spot right around now, and God knows he deserves it.

There you have it, a perfect example of what can be done once the awesome power of remote drones is added to your Bag of Death. The United States military uses drones, and they're really on to something with it. Since adopting their use, the number of times targets were hit in foreign countries without much international uproar is phenomenal. Send in the troops and everyone bitches, but send in the flying robots and everyone sort of goes "Meh." Now sure, if the authorities know it's you doing it they'll lock you up in a federal pound-me-in-the-ass prison (you aren't a government), but so long as you maintain proper operational security measures, when the fact of a bunch of dead neo-Nazis comes to light, the unofficial reaction will be "Meh."

So stock up the explosives, buy a few vans using false identities, and let the bodies hit the floor. ☺

Vehicle Selection:

This will be entirely dependent on your target area (rural, urban, dirt trails, etc.) and the size of explosive device being employed. An ATV with a gigantic steel canister on it will look extremely suspicious rolling down Wall Street in Manhattan; likewise, a low-rider Honda with carbon fiber body will suck at getting to a remote meth mega-lab in the backwoods of Kentucky. As with all things, try to match the situation to the most appropriate choice of tool.

You also aren't going to want a vehicle that attracts too much attention, so avoid snazzy sports cars or complete rust-buckets. Cars without drivers tend to get odd looks too—self-driving cars still aren't a common sight—so for city missions you'll likely be driving it to the vicinity prior to starting your remote bombing run. Hence, pay attention to all disguise essentials to avoid stupid mistakes.

Speaking of stupid mistakes, don't buy or rent vehicles using your real identity! Although this seems obvious, some vigilantes get too excited about the mission and then quit thinking properly. Make sure to wear solid disguises (silicone "faces" might be worth it); use fake identification and pay cash only. No paper trail that can lead to you. An even better option might be to steal a vehicle, especially if doing an out of town type of mission. Make sure to switch plates with one from your stock of decoys (note: accumulate a stock of decoy license plates), and then load it all up.

Due to the hassle with all of that, the remote controlled *ATV of Divine Retribution* might actually work best for most missions. Even in the city, you can roll up to an area within range, transporting it in a van;

then simply unload from the cargo hold and send it in on a robotic charge to glory. Most of your targets aren't going to be in nice, heavily trafficked parts of the city anyway, as crooks tend to stick to the fringes to avoid detention themselves. Wear your disguise anyway though, and employ decoy plates regardless.

The Nuts and Bolts of it All:

Yeah, I'm not going to run you through all of what's required; that could be an entire book in itself, full of diagrams, specifications and all kinds of shit. What I will do is let you know that the information is actually quite readily available, and a little internet searching will get you everything necessary. The great thing is that all those fools with too much time, money and stupidity on their hands have figured it all out for such moronic purposes as car surfing while driving with a smartphone app to control the mechanisms...I shit you not. We superheroes can turn this idiocy into crime-fighting mastery though, and we're even saved the hassle of figuring it out from scratch. So hug the next tech nerd you see for providing the mighty tools to destroy evil, even if it's only as a side-effect from their quest to escape boredom.

Now you have the main Weapons of Mass Awesomeness at your disposal, and already evil quakes with fear without realizing why. With potent explosive fury and the means to burn through solid steel, the arsenal is approaching completeness. But these **are** rather noticeable means of scum removal, and that's not always a good thing. What if there was a way to silently remove huge numbers of thugs at once with a colourless, tasteless substance that could fill an entire area in a comforting blanket of death? Well guess what, there is...read on.

{CHAPTER 18} CARBON MONOXIDE: KILLING SCUM IN DROVES

Imposing harsh Justice upon the world is an often messy business; blood, intestines, and scraps of ragged flesh litter the scene after many operations. This is especially true once bombs and incendiary devices are thrown into the mix. At times these are the best tools for the job—sometimes the only viable option—but it can get, well, just plain gross, to tell the truth. Wouldn't it be nice if an alternative method of scum removal existed, one which had great lethality but left bodies intact for cleaner, easy removal by the poor slob who gets stuck with that thankless job?

Luckily there is such an option, and it even gets around that little problem of building destruction...carbon monoxide! Yes, this wonder gas can provide the results you're looking for without many of the annoying issues. It is especially well suited to removing large groups of people in enclosed spaces, without them being any the wiser before they drop dead. Colourless, tasteless, and it presents no noticeable effects if the proper concentration is attained; people just quickly fall into a deep peaceful sleep from which they never awaken. At lower concentrations, death takes a bit longer, and certain symptoms may be noticeable (headache, dizziness, nausea). As a side benefit, unlike with bombs there's no damage to the building, cutting down on costly repairs for which insurance or local government would have to pay. Insurance payouts lead to premium increases, and government spending means tax increases, both of which only victimize the poor working stiffs who'd eventually end up footing the bill. That would be perpetrating an injustice if done without a damned good reason.

Another problem with bombs blowing things to bits in urban areas is the chance of innocent bystanders getting injured or killed. Now sure, in an abandoned factory housing a large-scale crack distribution hub this won't be such an issue, but in an occupied building this will fuck things up for the other residents. Carbon monoxide can be contained to a specific area by certain means though, and with the proper calculations ahead of time an amount which won't be lethal to the other residents in case of leakage can be brought (just enough for killing the target, with a slight reserve amount and no more).

In the following example, mentally substitute a bomb for the killing device after you've finished reading, and imagine the difference in collateral damage potential:

A janitor walks down the hotel hallway, pushing a cleaning cart loaded with supplies. Looking bored as fuck, he enters one of the cheaper conference rooms, there to make sure all garbages are empty and the paper products fully stocked. The catering staff had already set up a table with strong coffee and those terrible, rubbery sandwiches which seem to be the standard fare of such events. The attendees are already here, but nary a glance is sent his way; people do not notice those they dismiss as menial. Blending into the background as the first speaker starts to blab, he makes his way to a supply closet.

Still moving in a lackadaisical fashion, the janitor takes what looks like a compressed air tank from its hiding spot on the cart, places it in the closet and holds his breath as he turns the top valve almost full open, backing it off just enough to avoid too loud a hissing sound. The door is closed, and he steadily—but quickly—leaves the room, pushing the cart ahead while still holding his breath.

As the doors are closed a chunk of fast-drying epoxy putty gets placed between them...the two-part putty was mixed surreptitiously just prior to opening the valve (amazing what you can do when no one notices you). In a couple of minutes, the doors will not open without great effort, and may require a large pry-bar. The final thing to do before leaving is to seal the door sills bottom and top; this gets done by placing weather stripping in the gaps. The room is now rather sealed, to hold all the goodness inside. He walks away, with a smile growing across his face.

The room fills with a lethal concentration of carbon monoxide rather quickly. Once the target concentration is attained, unconsciousness takes only a few breaths; death follows in less than three minutes. On the path to lethal concentration, slight dizziness was felt, but not enough to cause alarm, especially because the target of 1.28 percent was quickly reached. But do not feel bad for the deceased, as they were a bunch of pedophile assholes, members of NAMBLA (North American Man/Boy Love Association). What a bunch of useless jerks... dead jerks now. ☺

No longer dressed as a janitor, a man walks by the hotel, stopping to check the time. When no one is looking he takes a pellet pistol fitted with a silencer from beneath his jacket, aims carefully, and sends a .22 caliber chunk of lead through the targeted window. The lethal gas is now free to dissipate so no innocent hotel workers get poisoned. Before anyone has even turned to look he is moving on, towards a well-deserved rest; maybe a good movie is showing at the theatre...

Now picture the devastation a large shrapnel bomb would have wreaked on the scene; for this operation, a simple tank of carbon monoxide was the perfect solution. Let's look at the checklist for when you should go with the same choice:

1) Large gathering of evil assholes in a confined area.
2) Other folks could become collateral damage if explosives or incendiaries were employed.
3) A relatively silent method of mass-extermination combined with almost zero property damage is the goal.

Okay, so we're all on board the Carbon Monoxide Express now—destination Justice—but just what is it about this snazzy gas that makes it so damn lethal? Well, prepare to have some knowledge mainlined straight to your cerebral cortex.

Carbon monoxide binds to hemoglobin much the same as oxygen does; hemoglobin is the stuff that makes your blood a useful way to transport oxygen from the lung absorption point throughout the entire body. The pertinent thing for our purpose is that carbon monoxide bonds <u>much</u> more strongly with hemoglobin than oxygen does, about **200 to 250 times** better than oxygen does, in fact (the older textbooks used to say 400 times better...whatever, it's a whole shitload more either way). This has the practical upshot that one can flood a confined space with a relatively minute amount of carbon monoxide and all the fuckwads in there will die.

We want combat effectiveness rather than a drawn-out thing they might escape, so aim to create a 1.28 percent concentration of carbon monoxide in the air. Such a concentration will cause unconsciousness after a few breaths, with death coming in about 3 minutes. If a tank large enough to reach that concentration is too bulky or heavy for use (might not be feasible to hide it given your mode of approach to the target), then a percentage of 0.64 percent will cause death in 20 minutes; there will be symptoms such as headache and dizziness in about a minute or two though, which might cause them to look for the source. At a 0.32 percent concentration death will come in 30 minutes, with symptoms after 5 to 10...this is only an option if you can ensure there's no chance of escape; in that case it could be funnier, as they'll suffer a bit before death takes them.

For the purposes of figuring most operations, though, aim at 1.28 percent; hence that's what will be aimed at in this example:

Explanatory Example: For this example, picture a room 14 meters long, 10 meters wide, and 3 meters in height. This equals 420 cubic meters of volume. One cubic meter equals 1000 liters; hence the volume of the space is 420000 liters. Dividing to get the 1.28 percent concentration of carbon monoxide gas needed gives an answer of 5376 liters. This can be compressed into about a 26.88 liter volume-by-water tank; a readily bought compressed gas cylinder with 29.5 liter-by-water volume is sized at 8 inches diameter and 48 inches long. So, if you can transport a tank of that size (and weight...it can get heavy), then you're good to go.

If you're going for a lower—yet still lethal—concentration, simply adjust the percentage in your calculations and work from there. The internet will make it relatively painless to find various sized tanks to fit all your death dealing needs. Different tank materials will operate at different pressures, and will weight significantly less (or more).

Obtaining Your Death Dealing Gas Supplies:

As with many other things, the internet really makes it all possible. There are various suppliers of carbon monoxide and suitable tanks due to the fact that it actually has many more uses than one might think at first glance.

Carboxymyoglobin is the stable compound formed when carbon monoxide and hemoglobin bind together. It gives a nice cherry red colour to your victim's corpses, but it also gives that pleasing colour to packaged meat, preventing the nasty brown colour it would otherwise be. It's also used for many chemical processes, as well as purifying nickel. Other uses exist but I won't bore you with them... the point is that there are legitimate, non-murder uses for it, which makes it available for sale.

But as with the case of buying gunpowder components, don't buy huge amounts all at once from one place, or the cops will be raiding your pad with the entire SWAT team in attendance once the bodies pile up. So be smart about buying, targeting, and how often you use it in any one location.

That wraps up what you need to know about carbon monoxide in a violent vigilante superhero context. Determine when it's appropriate, calculate your needs, and don't get stupid along the way. But you know what, these last few chapters have been pretty fucking grim. Scratch that, they've been a true donkey-raping downer at times; I mean, how much can you talk about blowing people up or shooting them in their testicles before it gets downright depressing, right?

Yeah, I know it's rough; I feel it too. Which is why we're switching gears right now and jetting off to a happy place. Pack all your troubles in your old kit bag...and then throw it in the ocean weighted down with a brick! It's time to cheer the fuck up.

{CHAPTER 19} MAINTAINING MORALE: KEEP FEELING SUPER!!!

Keeping one's morale up can be a difficult thing in this crazy world of turmoil. This is particularly true for those of us who take on the sometimes grim task of brutally beating the miscreants preying on society into submission. But it's not necessary to succumb to fits of brooding, soul-searching agony like Batman on a particularly bad day. Fuck no; in fact, crime-fighting should be cause for rejoicing, loudly announcing our glorious might to the world at large! Be more like unto The Tick, reveling in his invulnerability and ridiculous strength. Think super, act super, *be* super.

Part of this is remembering to reward yourself. Don't just put yourself on a pedestal...build that pedestal as well! Fill your surroundings with reminders of the obvious greatness you manifest. Celebrate each successful mission with a mighty feast (or at least a muffin). Instead of waffling about whether or not it's truly "necessary" at the moment, go ahead and purchase that kick-ass ballistic shield, even if it'll normally stay in the gear closet.

There is so much more to being a superhero than simply beating, clubbing and slashing one's way through a never-ending tide of criminal filth. Like a sage man once said, if it isn't fun, what's the point... so have fun with it! Go rappel down the side of a skyscraper for no reason at all; jump from rooftop to rooftop not out of considerations for secrecy, but just because you can. Celebrate your life's path, and make no apologies to anyone for it, especially yourself.

Even when engaged in serious matters, you'll be amazed at the huge differences small changes can make. Instead of using a baseball bat to give that vicious gang the beat-down, use a frozen Atlantic Cod. Instead of hurling teargas into a crowded criminal den, chuck in a nest of angry hornets. Rather than using throwing stars to aid in strategic getaways, sharpen up a batch of those horrible cookies your mother-in-law inflicts on everyone each Christmas. Trust me, when you're beating a crime-boss into unconsciousness with a dried length of deli meat, an unstoppable smile will light up your face. ☺

Never lose sight of why you got into this in the first place...adventure. Sure, it's also about making the world a better place, blah blah blah, but deep down a huge part of it involves imposing your indomitable, glorious will upon the world at large. The fact that it benefits mankind as well is simply further testimony to undeniable greatness; proclaim that greatness! It is yours by right, it is yours by might; even if the public remains kept in the dark about exactly who keeps the city safe, the glory is no less.

There is, however, something to be said for leaving a tangible legacy, an epic record which chronicles the rise to glory along with all the rest. I'm talking about something grand here, the creation of a legend. Join the ranks of Beowulf, Thor, King Arthur and all those other mighty Heroes who form the very archetypes we base the entire concept upon. Fashion your exploits into a mythology, an inspiring, cohesive and exciting tale of prevailing against mighty odds...and looking good while doing it too.

And as a special bonus, I'll even teach you how to write it in such a manner that you'll not see prison time due to stupidly publishing incriminating evidence. Learn how to craft the often disjointed series of events our journals end up as into a tale which will be sung around the campfire for generations to come. *You* already know you are great; it's time for the rest of the world to know it as well.

{CHAPTER 20} WRITING YOUR LEGACY: SUPERHERO MEMOIRES

Some folks would question the very notion of creating the chronicle which establishes your legacy of greatness. They might trot out some psychological mumbo jumbo full of concepts they generally don't even understand in a vain attempt to lend credibility to their defense of mediocrity. The truth of it is that when stripped of its verbal camouflage, the argument against boils down to a single word; "Why?"

"Why not?" is the simplest answer, and truthfully it is the only one they merit or have any chance of comprehending. They pretend to be content in a life of mundane nothingness, trying with all their might to brainwash themselves into truly believing the lie they live every single day. But we know better; life is an adventure, and you have to grip the bull by the horns and wrestle reality into a suitable shape. Writing your own legend is part of this process.

You see, although the masses are living a lie, they are able to form a semblance of reality through consensus of sheer numbers. This _Consensus Reality_ is part of what we must overcome on our rise to the heights of superheroism. For although the reality formed by mass consensus is mainly psychological (with possible quantum mechanical effects...the jury is still out on that), it affects all beings raised under its spell. You are born and raised into believing certain things, and it takes great strength of will to break away from that conditioning. Moreover, even once on the path to greatness, the influence of the masses reaches out to try and entangle you again, enforcing a boring, mundane view of what is possible.

So we proclaim our triumphs, and rage against the limitations those weaklings attempt to impose upon us! Through the exercising of our will, we begin to untangle the web of limitations; through the act of focusing and distilling our efforts over time, our own consensus reality is built. For as a society of one possesses the same legitimacy as a society of billions, so too does a *consensus of one* act to influence reality (at least psychologically...and possibly on other levels as mentioned before; who knows).

Besides, it's great fun seeing your heroic legacy forming exactly as you choose. ☺

Plus, another great truth people forget is that if *you* don't write the story of your life, someone else will...and they are probably stupid as well as disinterested. Fuck that noise.

Superhero Language: Emphasize for Effect:

Get into the habit of using superhero ways of writing, especially in creating your chronicle. You've probably noticed how Justice is always capitalized in this book; that is no accident. Big concepts like **Justice, Truth**, and **Retribution** are great words to capitalize, adding emphasis. For one thing, it adds importance to them, reminding everyone of just how pertinent they truly are; just look to how religions employ the same tactic (God is always capitalized in Christianity). By seeding your reality with constant reminders of what is most important, the Mission will always remain foremost in your thoughts.

Another way of doing this is with descriptors; the fight wasn't *okay*, it was *glorious*. Words like *scum-rot savage* have far more visceral impact than saying "The criminal wasn't very nice." One term grips you by the guts, inciting feelings of Heroic Rage, while the other wording makes you say "Meh." Instead of front kicks, try *destructive stomping kicks of Brutal Vengeance*. Describe things with terms like *vile, heroic, overwhelming,* and other words that differentiate between the existence most people plod through as opposed to the grand adventure you live every single day.

Don't hesitate to switch up the way normal things—such as coffee— are portrayed in your glorious chronicle. You didn't merely drink a coffee, oh no; you imbibed an herbal energy elixir to prepare for battle, prepared according to an ancient procedure handed down for generations. Grocery shopping becomes stocking up on disaster preparedness supplies; going to the gym translates as engaging in a superhero strength maintenance regimen; sewing torn cargo pants is actually super-suit repair...I think you're beginning to see the point. When even everyday activities can be transformed on the page into acts of adventure, you'll have no problems in finding the proper wording to describe mighty battles against the very real evil which stalks in the night. It will also help to keep the appropriate level of enthusiastic optimism towards the heroic life; a happy, well-adjusted vigilante is far more effective than a bitter, tortured soul full of pent-up rage (unpent that rage on the violent savages roaming the streets instead, then write about it).

Invoke the Gods:

People call upon God for all sorts of crap all the time; a raise; that promotion; winning the lottery...I'm not talking about any of that shit. Nor am I referring to asking God for success or inspiration in writing. What I am speaking of is bringing reference to the gods cultures throughout the ages have worshipped into your legend; weave their legacy into yours.

By sprinkling references to Thor, Odin, Ganesh, Shiva and assorted others, those reading your words will subconsciously confer the mighty attributes of those deities to whatever you connect their names with. For instance, when you "Hurled my hammer forcefully into his face like the mighty Norse god Thor himself", the reader immediately ascribed all sort of awesome characteristics unto you. You are mighty, brave, and nigh immortal as well; that's the power of such a linkage.

It works well when describing your enemies as well. You see, people will get bored if you just shot another crack-head in the face, but when the villain "Has the duplicitous cunning of the trickster god Loki" it's a whole other story. The reader is drawn into the tale, waiting with bated breath to see how such a potent adversary was bested. You can always go with the generic description of *demonic* for some foes, but to truly craft a legend to resound throughout the ages, go with "name brand deities" that embody the exact qualities you wish to portray.

This strategy also works when referring to objects, tools/weapons and vehicles; "A hammer fit for a Norse god"; "This blade could slay a frost giant"; a gun could be said to possess the destructive fury of Shiva, destroyer of worlds...things of that nature. Just remember not to describe every single little thing with such terminology, lest the effect be lost through overuse.

Keep Your Ass Out of Prison:

Alright, so you want to get your story out there to the masses; you have enough exploits to fill an entire book; you've learned the knack for superhero verbiage and have an encyclopedic knowledge of gods from four different cultures, including all the mighty traits they're noted for. It's time to slap it all together and submit for publication, right? Well, answer this question first: do you enjoy prison cuisine and getting intimate in the shower room over a bar of dropped soap? If the answer is no, then you'd best keep reading.

You see, an unabridged accounting of your exploits is any district attorney's wet dream. Every "criminal" act you've ever committed (they don't see things our way), every instance of premeditation, it's all there in black and white, worded for extreme readability and excitement; the jury won't even get bored and drift off while the D.A. gleefully destroys you in court. This is obviously not what one likely intends to be the outcome of recounting their majestic war on evil, so steps must be taken to avoid such an ignoble ending.

Thus, there's only one thing to do; fictionalize. Be like those television documentaries where "The names and certain events have been changed in order to protect the innocent." That's exactly what the fuck I'm talking about! They switch shit up enough that people are able to keep living peacefully afterwards instead of being cut up for fish bait by organized crime, yet retain enough "truthiness" to still call it a documentary.

You're going to go one better and call the **whole thing** fictional. Certain facts will be altered to protect the innocent (mainly you, in this case), and then the claim will be made that *none* of it is true. Yet it won't matter one bit in the final analysis as regards the original intent for the chronicle. You see, over time facts tend to blur anyway, and what was true gets thought of as false, while certain bits of pure fiction get remembered as 100 percent, unadulterated truth. Most things from the past get lumped in the middle ground, and people just cannot remember for the life of them what the actual truth of it is.

So feel free to change names, dates, numbers of people involved... hell, locate the action on another continent even! The important thing is that the *story* be sufficiently entertaining to persist. Tell people an inspiring tale of triumph over insurmountable odds and history will judge you well. Let the songs of the far future be about ***The Canadian Crusader, Furious Butcher of Villainy*** (or whatever your name is); let the children of that distant era pattern their conceptions of bravery and Honour upon your grand legacy.

You are now armed with the literary tools required to create the testament to your amazing greatness. The proper way to describe things tempered with the wisdom to avoid annoying incarceration issues has been imparted, and the future is already looking more super.

But you know something, as important as natural talent, dedication and the proper attitude are to success in our crime-fighting enterprise, it sure would be easier to accomplish the mighty tasks before us if actual superpowers were possessed, wouldn't it? Can't you just imagine the advantage of stronger muscles and tendons, denser bones and reduced healing time? Wouldn't it be awesome if there was a real-life super-soldier serum available to give nature the middle finger? Can you feel the *yearning* to transcend genetically imposed limitations?

Well get ready to jump into a new mindset in your newly transformed body then! It's time to rise; it's time to be more than ever before; it's time to get some motherfucking superpowers. ☺

{CHAPTER 21} HEROIC NUTRITION: YOUR PATH TO SUPERPOWERS

Too many folks have been brainwashed into the mindset that that the way you are "naturally" is the optimal form. Perhaps some strength training and cardio workouts can be thrown into the mix, but anything beyond that and a multivitamin, forget it; totally unnecessary.

Well, this might be sufficient for the teeming masses who never test themselves with anything more strenuous in their daily life than lifting a cappuccino or fixing a paper-jam in the office printer. If they're buying into the limited—extremely limited—options the so-called "real world" sanctions, then sure, exceeding the limitations of "normal" biology may hold no appeal or even much benefit. But as we are on a different path—*a super path*—much more is required.

Just think about it for a moment, and the benefits for the crime-fighting superhero become crystal clear. It's easy enough to load up with body armour weighing 80 to 100 pounds total when crafting a super-suit capable of protecting the entire body from practically all handheld threats, including high-powered rifles. On top of that you could add another 40 pounds of gear and weaponry, if going balls-to-the-wall with it. That's going to take some serious strength to move effectively in; good luck with that if you don't surpass the common man (or woman). Or even if that type of heroics isn't your cup of tea, consider the rather immense weight of a large fragmentation bomb, or even a decent size gas cylinder of carbon monoxide, especially when fully loaded. Some of the shit we do takes lots of strength.

Even if you're the parkour, fly through the air type of hero you'll benefit from greater strength, stronger tendons/ligaments and denser bones; muscles will propel to new heights, while bones and tendons absorb shock from landing. Truthfully, unless you're strictly a cyber-ninja who stalks scum purely through electronic means, extra strength will supercharge your heroics' every aspect. Even if the plan is to be a fat blob of a hero, choose to be a **strong** fat blob of a hero.

So without further ado, let's get super!

Steroids:

I can already hear the cries of anguish as legions of folks squirm in their seats; "Steroids, aren't those the bad things that people use to cheat at sports, then die from liver failure after?" Well, sort of, almost, but not really...bear with me here.

Steroids are simply hormones the body produces and uses to regulate a wide range of biological functions. For instance, testosterone is a steroid your body produces which prevents osteoporosis, increases bone mass, and stimulates muscle growth (it's produced mainly in the testicles for men, and the ovaries in women). Birth control pills are a synthetic hormone, and cortisone has eased the horrid, debilitating joint pains of countless thousands. So before you go around bad mouthing steroids, remember that you're already full of them, and they serve valid medical uses.

What most folks are talking about when discussing the evils of performance enhancing hormones are anabolic steroids. These are largely based on replicating (or improving upon) the muscle building and strength enhancing qualities of testosterone, and they sure do work in that regard. They do also have a host of side effects which will be discussed along the way, but their main side effect is greatness! Heroic size, amazing strength, increased endurance and reduced recovery time...this is exactly the sort of thing we see in comic book heroes *all the time*; why *wouldn't* you want such an advantage? What possible crime-fighting disadvantage is there in lifting more, punching harder, leaping higher and running faster?

Besides, if you end up with a failing liver 37 years from now, so what? That just gives a great excuse to buy that awesome new bionic liver, beginning the transformation into an even more potent engine of destruction! Pair that snazzy new bionic liver with some bionic lungs...add some flame-resistant skin...perhaps some nano-tube lattice-work bones are in order...the sky's the limit. ☺

Anadrol: This is one of the strongest of the orally administered steroids, with many people seeing 10 to 15 pounds of extra size within a couple of weeks. Besides providing an enormous increase in strength levels, the water retention effects of it make extreme exertion easier on the joints. Red blood cell count goes up as well, which translates into more oxygen transport capacity; this gives greater endurance, allowing for the pummeling of plenty more bad guys in a row.

Dosage is somewhere around 0.8 mg per pound of your body mass, taken every day. Duration of use should not exceed cycles of 5 to 6 weeks. Some other steroid—or other mass-preserving measure—needs to be started as one goes off of it, lest the gains disappear almost as quickly.

Stacks well with Deca-Durabolin, and maintaining the Deca as one cycles off the Anadrol should fight muscle atrophy. Adding hCG as well when cycling off will get those testicles back in order; make them pull their weight in the muscle maintenance arena.

It is also, unfortunately, one of the worst for liver-toxic side effects. It is also strongly contraindicated for women, so superheroines should not choose this option.

Anavar (Oxandrolone): This steroid was initially developed for use with women or children, and is noted for having almost no incidences of side effects when using anywhere near a sane dosage. It isn't the most anabolic (muscle-building), but does result in great increases in strength. It also doesn't affect the body's own production of testosterone, so you're simply adding greatness to your naturally occurring might.

It makes a great combo with Deca-Durabolin; to calculate the Anavar dosage, simply use the figure of 0.125 mg per pound of body mass.

It is a daily dosage type of steroid, and mixes well with Anadrol if you don't mind liver failure far in advance of bionic replacement options.

Deca-Durabolin: Developed in the 1960's, this injectable steroid is still immensely popular for its mostly positive results compared with some other options. It does a great job of maintaining a positive nitrogen balance in the muscle cells, thus potentiating muscle growth. Great for building muscle mass as well as easing joint pain... no wonder it is a fan favourite.

Dosage is generally in the 200 to 600 mg per week range; above that you get more side effects, without much increase in anabolic activity. Most men go for around 400 mg per week...you may wish to go with 600 as maximizing strength is the goal here. Women who don't go above 100 mg per week seem to have no issues, but jump up to a higher dosage if an enlarged clit doesn't bother you.

It is one of the best steroids for mix-and-match muscle-blasting fun!

Dianabol: This is another oral steroid with big mass-building delivery; during the first 6 weeks you can get up to 4 pounds of extra muscle each week. It also deposits extra calcium in the bones! 15-50 mg per day is the normal dosage range, with most folks not venturing above 40. Ten weeks is about the maximum sane cycle length; exceed at your own risk.

Can be stacked with Deca-Durabolin or Anavar; don't try it with Anadrol.

Human Chorionic Gonadotropin (hCG): This is a natural hormone which develops in the human placenta of pregnant women; it is manufactured for consumption from their urine.

"Eww!!!" some of you will undoubtedly say, but listen up on what it does for you. You see, men tend to get the shrunken balls from many steroid cycles, due to the old testicles not having to produce any testosterone of their own. What hCG does is kick them back into action, which has the practical upshot of not losing much of that glorious muscle you worked so hard to get. Some people start injecting it during their cycle, while others wait till they're about to cycle off; that's up to you.

Dosage is one ampule injected every 5 days; each ampule is 5000 IU (international units).

Human Growth Hormone (HGH): This is a great one, as it can actually cause muscular hyperplasia, which is an actual increase in the number of muscle cells. Steroids alone cannot do this; they can only cause an increase in muscle cell size (hypertrophy). HGH also results in muscular hypertrophy, so it's all good. Beyond that, HGH strengthens tendons, cartilage and other connective tissues...you'll get stronger, denser bones too. In addition, the gains tend to be kept after use is discontinued.

It doesn't do it all on its own though; you need to add steroids, thyroid hormones, and a whole bunch of protein (protein is needed with the steroids alone anyway, though). Some folks add insulin injections into the mix, but that's pretty stupid and needlessly risky, even for us; just eat 6-7 meals a day and you'll be fine.

Dosage is about 0.3 IU per pound of body mass per week. The manufacturers suggest taking that in 3 injections over the course of a week, but some people break it up into multiple times per day injections due to the very short half-life of HGH (one hour or less). The liver might do better with these smaller amounts per injection.

Cytomel: It's a synthetic thyroid hormone; take it along with your HGH. Dosage is 100 mcg per day tops; start at 25 mcg per day.

*Your recommended course of action: I'm going to recommend a regular cycling of 600 mg per week of Deca-Durabolin with 50 mg per day of Anavar. Go with cycles of 10 to 12 weeks on the juice, starting the hCG injections about 1 to 2 weeks before the cycle ends. Cut the hCG after 3 weeks; your balls should be good to go. Many folks say to cycle off for at least the same length of time as you're on, but in the interest of becoming superhuman I'll say 6 weeks off before starting up again.

If you go the human growth hormone route as well, you might want to take longer breaks between cycles and get some liver function tests...or just blast ahead and say fuck the risks! Either way is cool. Don't forget your thyroid hormone supplements to get the most out of the HGH and steroid stacking fun.

Women should probably stick with 20 mg of Anavar stacked with 200 mg of Deca-Durabolin; that'll ramp up your strength levels beyond what most large men can reach naturally, even with lots of quality time at the gym. But if you're willing to hero-the-fuck-up and throw caution to the wind, I honestly salute you...just use the larger male recommended dosages and get ready to pull the arms off of evil!

Protein:

But no matter how much steroids you gobble up and inject, the gains won't come without the proper muscular building blocks. The main thing you need to increase your intake of is protein, loads and loads of protein.

Most people are "protein wimps", constantly under-consuming; no wonder they're so weak. A sedentary office worker could get by with 0.5 grams per pound of body mass, and many don't even get that much. As you're going to be performing mighty acts of Justice on an ongoing basis, ever increasing in intensity, a target of at least one gram of protein per pound of body mass will be required. When at the heights of steroid fueled working out, you may be able to utilize 1.5 grams per pound of mass; beyond that isn't going to do much.

Red meat, fish and egg whites are good sources (and you'll want to eat them all), but the best way to up your intake is with protein shakes; you want the whey protein. People sometimes argue about whether to go with protein isolate versus concentrate; isolate absorbs quicker, whereas concentrate digests a bit more slowly... the main thing is quantity, so don't sweat it. The ladies going on the

Retribution Rampage may want to include a fair bit of soy based protein shakes...it is supposed to have some good side benefits for issues women sometimes get stuck with. Men can have a bit of soy based stuff, but should limit it.

Beans are another source of protein, and 12 grain bread has surprising amounts, more than you'd expect; both will help keep your fiber levels up so you don't end up full of shit. Besides, you need something to act as a side dish. Speaking of side dishes, that leads into the next section!

Carbs:

Forget the Atkins Diet; you need carbs, especially when you're running around town breaking heads. With this in mind, why not start your day with oatmeal, to get those nice complex carbohydrates for long-lasting energy. Whole grains (wheat, rice, barley, oats), beans and vegetables are your key foods to getting the carbs you need. Potatoes and pasta are good for it as well.

Fats:

Don't avoid fats either. Your body will need a certain amount to work as building materials along with protein for the steroids/HGH, and they also provide great long lasting energy. In the form of mixed (unsalted) nuts they'll provide portable, easily eaten energy on-the-go. Have some eggs with the yolks along with the morning oatmeal and keep going for hours. Beef has some useful fat along with that protein you seek...fish has oily fats good for heart health as well as energy...fight crime with fat!

Vitamins and Minerals:

When you're building a superior body, you need more of just about everything. Muscles, bones and connective tissues all require more supplemental nutrition than be found in food alone. All your extra working out on top of the crime-fighting activities at the heart of it all will up the need for anti-oxidants as well.

Luckily, multi-vitamins have come a long way over the years, so a Centrum Forte along with a Stresstab will cover the basics, freeing you to simply substitute the extras (Stresstab has all the B vitamins needed and then some). The following vitamin and mineral dosage are aimed at bodybuilders, who have similar needs to us:

1) Vitamin C=> 3000-6000 mg per day
2) Vitamin D=> 1000 IU per day
3) Vitamin E=> 1000 IU per day
4) Calcium=> 2600 mg per day
5) Magnesium=> 600-800 mg per day
6) Iron=> 60 mg per day
7) Phosphorus=> 1200 mg per day

You can also add some glucosamine to the overall mix as a joint support supplement; it should help fight the wear and tear on your cartilage. Some folks say that glucosamine hydrochloride may work better than the more commonly found sulfate, but it's a matter of debate. Dosages of 1000 to 2000 mg per day are not unheard of; adjust the amount taken to suit your individual needs.

That's the major info you need in order to construct a supplement and diet plan capable of transformation from the merely human into the superhuman. Become your own mad scientist, and unleash the results of that experimentation upon the city's underworld. Rampage as an unstoppable juggernaut of Brutal Justice, and rack up the body count as a wave of fear robs your enemies' will before battle is yet joined.

But before you reap the fruits of your steroid fueled labours, the ground must be properly prepared. We're not sowing seeds of corn, however, oh no; we're sowing the seeds of Retribution, and the water they require can only be found at the gym. Next up: *Pumping Iron*.

{CHAPTER 22} "THAT'S IT, JUST GIVE ME ANOTHER HALF-MILLION REPS...": SUPERHERO STRENGTH REGIMEN

"Crap, just one foot more...!" (As he falls to the ground far below the rooftop not quite leapt to)

"Can't...quite...reach...that...lever..." (Trapped under a measly 3 thugs)

"If only that punch had landed with more force; **FUCK!!!**" (Said moments before losing consciousness due to a choke hold he lacked the strength to escape from)

Face it; we heroes have more at stake than most folks much of the time. If the average slob lacks the requisite strength, he might need to ask for help hefting that box. If his back gets strained, a sick day may be order. If <u>your</u> strength fails you, death could be the result; perhaps many deaths, depending on the mission.

So don't fuck around and waste your time with a goddamned Bowflex! You made the right decisions about so many things, including the choice to chemically augment biology in order to transcend normal physical limits; keep on the right track to maximize greatness. With the correct exercise regimen, Batman won't have shit on you; 600 pound bench press; 1200 pound leg presses for multi-rep sets with ease. You'll be the guy at the gym searching for bigger dumbbells than are commercially available.

But it ain't gonna happen till you start hitting those weights...along with some other stuff as well. The end goal is slightly different than the usual gym-rat; you're a violent superhero, viciously imposing your own brand of Justice, remember? So inject some Deca-Durabolin and wash down that Anavar with a triple espresso, because it's go time. ***Rahhhrrrgh!!!***

Build Strength Fast! Compound Motion:

The core of your rise to crazy new heights of strength will consist of compound motion exercises. You're not in this to win a beauty contest; you're in it to develop the strength needed to pull a head clean off! Isolation exercises will still play a part, but these exercises will form the base to build from.

Deadlifts: "I lift things up and put them down"...that pretty much sums up this exercise. Deadlifts recruit an insane number of muscle groups into a deceptively simple motion. Make sure to use proper form and keep your lower back good and straight, lest you become ***Spasm Man, Amazing Swallower of Powerful Pain Meds.*** If you do it right though, the release of extra growth hormone will be a great boon to muscle growth, and result in a back capable of supporting truly heroic levels of exertion.

Squats: Generations of strength coaches have said "If you want your arms to grow, squat!" This exercise also increases levels of growth hormone; plus, it blasts the legs and ass like nothing else can. Once again, proper form is key to avoiding idiotic back injuries, so do it right for fuck's sake. Perform it with heavier and lighter weights, varying reps and speed of performance. Develop legs of steel that can kick, stomp and leap with explosive power.

Bench Press: The gold standard for strength; when people ask how strong you are, they generally mean how much can be benched. Although some folks argue that it serves no real-life purpose, they're simply wrong, so we'll happily ignore the nonsense they spew. ☺ Perform it at all different angles; flat, incline and decline. Switch it up between dumbbells and barbells, to increase strength in stabilizing muscles as well as straight-up maximum one-rep power. Vary the weights, reps and sets; use heavier and lighter weights; do it fast as well as slow. When done right, you'll increase both your explosive punching power as well as the endurance-style strength needed for grappling combat needs.

Rows: Cable rows, bent-over rows, and one-arm rows...do them all. Jump on those machines that get rows going at odd angles (Hammer Strength makes some good ones); rows are simply bench presses for your back. You want to balance out your forward and backward smashing power, so get on it already! Same thing about varying weights/reps/sets and speed of performance; develop strength **and** power.

Pull-downs: This is the same motion as with chin-ups/pull-ups, simply with a machine instead. The machine allows for use of weights more than you weigh, as well as the option for using decreasing weights to keep the exercise going to muscular exhaustion. Remember to do wide-grip and close-grip variations, as well as palms inward and neutral grip to target all muscle groups possible.

Clean and Press: Lift the weight off the ground, then press it over your head. You're doing exercises that push forward, pull backward and down as well; makes sense to push upward too. Do it with both barbells and dumbbells; follow the same guidelines as the other exercises as regards mixing things up.

Isolation Exercises:

Although compound motions will do the most to build full-body strength, you'll still want to balance things out and augment certain areas; that's where isolation exercises come in. As they name implies, these are exercises that *isolate* specific muscles in order to target them specifically.

Curls: Do them with barbells and dumbbells. Preacher curls; reverse curls; concentration curls...do them while standing, sitting, or with specific benches designed for such things. Cable curls, hammer curls, the list goes on. Rotate through most of them for full biceps development, as well as to prevent tendon issues (repetitive stress injuries).

Triceps Extensions: Basically the opposite of curls; you extend your arm instead of bending it. Cables, dumbbells, barbells, machines... it's all good.

And the Rest: Shoulder raises; hip abductor/adductor; leg extensions; leg curls...fuck, do you want me to do them for you also? Just go to the gym already; it ain't rocket science!

Exercise Your Core:

If you don't have a strong core (abs, obliques and such), the full power of punching and kicking will forever remain elusive. Hence, work it out; sit-ups, Roman chair, side bends with weight and leg raises should do it. If you're a trendy sort of dude, throw in some planks for good measure. Back extensions will help to round it all out; simply sprinkle these exercises in between the main strength builders.

Cardio:

Run to or from the gym (or both); ride a bike if that's too far. The rest of your cardio needs should be met by stalking through the night; save time at the gym for weights. If you really feel the *need* for gym based cardio though, use the elliptical and jack-up the resistance for a grueling full-body workout.

Heavy Bag:

You should be hitting the bag during martial arts training, but why not bash it some more while at the gym, right? As a handy bonus, you'll be wearing shoes or boots at the gym, providing for the street clothes practice that most dojos have a severe allergy to.

Superhero-Specific Exercises:

NOW we reach the part of it where most personal trainers wouldn't have a clue. Some trainers for strongman competitions and MMA would be on the right track, but would likely forget a few things all the same. Luckily, I'm here to fill you in on what exercise books neglect; so put on your heaviest body armour, and let's get started!

"Batman Kicks": These are for when you want to throw a dynamic double-leg kick into a villain's face with the assistance of a handy tree or fire escape ladder. As a side benefit, they work grip strength and the abs. When at the gym, simply grab the chin-up bar, then pull slightly upward with your arms, tense the abs to raise the legs and snap/stomp the feet out forcefully. Return to starting position and repeat. If the set-up is correct, get a running start before grabbing the bar; consider wearing ankle weights to simulate heavy boots, if your gym is one of those namby-pamby "health club" ones which prohibit the wearing of heavy boots.

Also perform this exercise in the great outdoors anytime you run across a handy tree or fire escape ladder. Wear your heaviest body armour whenever weather permits its concealment, and get out there; if you're *really* lucky, perhaps a criminal will be found along the way for some bonus bashing workout fun.

Full Armour Rope Climb: What good is it if you can only slide down a rope? That's a step in the right direction, but it's only halfway there. Consider also this simple question: do you fight crime while in the nude? If you don't fight nude, then this exercise is for you! Get all geared up in the heaviest load-out you possess; then head out there, set the rope up and get to climbing. As trees provide great rope anchoring potential, you'll get to practice tree climbing while geared up as well, which is a handy skill to have. You haven't felt your lats burn in a big way till you try this out.

Stair Climbing with a Sack o' Rocks: Climbing stairs is easy once you're in shape; climbing 8 flights over and over with a sack of rocks on your back is hard. Strap on a backpack with 60 to 80 pounds of rocks in it, then go up and down the stairs till your legs give out. The pack can be taken off in between "sets" as a break; it feels a lot lighter with the rocks off, and no one is going to steal it anyway (especially since it's recommended to use a really shitty backpack due to wear and tear from rocks).

This will kill your legs more than you can imagine, and will prepare for rescue or assault missions. You can substitute a weighted vest for the sack o' rocks, but there's something inherently more hard-core and awesome about the old-school way...feels more gritty and brutal somehow.

Sledgehammers and Axes: MMA fighters often pound huge tractor tires with sledgehammers to help build <u>functional strength</u> of the sort used for various punching and bashing applications. You need this also so by all means follow their example. However, you're going to levels of brutal extremity beyond anything Chuck Liddell or any of the rest are, so something additional is required.

When one considers that hammers and axes are great for imposing Justice through bodily damage AND bashing/cutting through obstacles cowardly criminals hide behind, the answer is obvious: bash everything you possibly can with sledgehammers and axes! Is there a boarded-up house nearby, or possibly an abandoned factory? That could be a great place to start; chop through walls, break wire-reinforced glass; why not practice your door-kicking skills while there (it sure helped me out in my quests)?

The woods are another great exercise arena; find huge deadwood logs/fallen trees and hack them apart as if they were child molesters. Then, hurl the dismembered chunks through the air, developing yet more functional strength that will come in handy. And if you're really lucky, you'll stumble across a meth lab! Yay!!!

Training Schedule:

With all the steroids and supplementation doing their thing, it should be possible to maintain a 6 day per week workout schedule, alternating between upper body and lower body days. If you start feeling symptoms of overtraining, back off a tad; a day off now and then won't fuck things up...just don't wimp out (as a superhero, I know you'll do the right thing). It is also possible that at times a workout may have to be toned down or skipped for particularly vigorous crime elimination missions. This is okay, so don't sweat it; cortisol is a stress hormone with annoying catabolic (muscle destroying) effects, so by getting all worried about such shit you'd actually end up making it even worse. Just take any frustrations out on the nearest mugger or rapist, and think happy thoughts. ☺

Whew, that'll get you started on the path to mega-strength in a hurry, especially as the weights used continue to climb ever higher. Just try to ignore the stares from curious folks at the gym, and don't scare them too much if they're a tad annoying at times; remember, only smash criminals, no matter how much the rage builds from having 100 times the normal testosterone level coursing through your veins! The Hulk was mighty, but he raged too damn much...and never got invited to parties. Just think of that (and the total lack of sex which might result) when puny humans get on your magnificent nerves.

A certain part from this section leads to another hero lesson though, one which will lead into a couple of chapters. Remember the humble backpack stuffed with rocks, and how handy it was for building massive leg endurance? It's also great for carrying lots of other stuff too; let's take a closer look at common items which can serve our heroic needs without attracting too much unwanted attention.

{CHAPTER 23} BACKPACKS INSTEAD OF BAT-BELTS: UTILITY YOU CAN WEAR...ANYWHERE

Let me tell you a tale of two heroes.

Hero #1:

He wakes up mere hours before the sun goes down; night is when the worst of the scum crawl out of their holes to plague the city. Grimly he eats his "breakfast" of oatmeal and eggs...even the tasty bacon on the side doesn't put a smile on this crime-fighter's face; Justice is serious business, and a momentary slip-up could easily spell death. So he eats in silence, as the dots on the interactive crime map which constantly fills one of the computer monitors forms a meditative background, influencing tonight's patrol route choice.

After completing the necessary hygienic routine, protective gear gets fitted on overtop the black Nomex under-suit. Utility belt: check. Weaponry in place: check. Emergency first aid kit: check. All systems go; time to put the ballistic mask on and hit the streets.

As he walks down a side street after exiting an alley only a few blocks from his residence, a patrol car rounds the corner; fellow crime-fighters in a different uniform, working long hours to keep the streets safe. The hero keeps on walking...only to be blinded as a high-intensity search light is trained on his face. The officers leap out of the car after screeching to a halt, shouting commands to drop to the ground with hands where they can see them! Don't they know he's a hero, that he walks a parallel path to theirs?!?

The police book him back at the station, receiving congratulations from their captain for removing a dangerous criminal from the night-time streets. That heavily armed and armoured maniac was obviously going

153

to murder a whole lot of innocent people, and probably anticipated a shootout with police given the type of gear he was caught with. His cover story about being a "superhero" is dismissed as total bullshit, a ploy to try for an insanity plea.

Hero #2:

A man walks down the street, dressed in black cargo pants and a dark green T-shirt. He has a smile on his face and is wearing a dark green backpack as well. The sun has set and the night-time thugs will soon be out and about, but this city traveler looks completely unconcerned, serene even. No one looks twice in his direction, except for the ubiquitous prostitutes looking for those cruising in search of dirty sex.

As he exits an alley and heads down a less travelled side street, a police patrol car rounds the corner. They continue on down the street, cruising the city streets in search of criminals who might prey upon those such as the guy just passed.

No one suspects the truth; this man is a seasoned crime-fighting vigilante, and the backpack contains a ballistic mask; .357 Magnum revolver; extendable baton; first aid kit; rope; handcuffs, etc. It even has a ballistic plate in the rear compartment capable of taking strikes from multiple rifle rounds, making it capable of use as a shield if need be.

At a nearby coffee shop he grabs a chocolate dip donut and a coffee with two espresso shots; it's a good night to be alive.

So, which hero do <u>you</u> want to be, eh?

I get it; I understand the urge to stalk through the night in full superhero get-up, I really do. There are times it is permissible or even advantageous to do so, and such situations have been listed along the way...but sometimes you really need to blend in with the crowd. To take a lesson from another hero's journal, *you are* the hero; it is your true self. All the body armour, masks and other stuff are simply tools, chosen to make the missions you engage in successful; if you lose sight of that, failure will be the result rather than the glory so rightly desired (and deserved). So don't overlook the tactical advantage simple choices can provide.

Case in point is the humble backpack. ☺ It offers all the gear carrying capacity of a utility belt (and then some), but doesn't give the total freak look to any onlooker in the vicinity. The only down side is in deployment speed, but for many missions that will be fully offset by the *not getting arrested on the way there* aspect. Besides, the two are not mutually exclusive; a utility belt can be shoved in the pack as well...just gear up prior to entering combat.

A backpack can easily contain the following:

1) 30 feet of sturdy rope
2) A large revolver or semi-auto pistol with holster and extra ammo
3) Bullet-resistant clipboard or Kevlar/steel/titanium bullet-resistant plate
4) Water and food to help fuel patrols
5) Compact pry-bar and bolt cutters
6) Ballistic mask
7) Gloves, cloth face mask, a shirt

Plus other assorted things, depending on individual bag capacity and weight considerations.

I have found that the low-key approach allows for better surveillance opportunities as well, while still being able to get ready for action in a decent amount of time. It is possible that you may wish to go even "lower-key" at times though; sometimes having a .50 caliber Desert Eagle in your bag can be a liability. You might also be headed to places where guns are a no-no; it is possible that the hunt for slimy criminal bastards could lead to lands such as Australia where even a normal knife could fuck things up. Or maybe you just want the ability to check out a museum exhibit after bashing thugs' skulls in, and weapons aren't allowed on the premises. The reason isn't my concern...hey, it's your life! So I'm just going to drop the knowledge on you, sanguine with the fact that it'll be put to good use. Go stab a rapist in the eye with a pencil; you'll be glad you did.

{CHAPTER 24} "AND A PEN WHICH CAN BE DRIVEN THROUGH A SKULL..." EVERYDAY ITEMS THAT CAN SERVE DOUBLE DUTY

What could possibly be more low-key than a pen? We often have them with us, whether at work, school, or just for signing papers at the bank (their pens are *gross*). You can even carry one into a courthouse or onto an airplane. No one *ever* says "Oh my God, he has a pen! We're all going to die!!!" You'll never hear that phrase anywhere other than in this book.

Yet the tactical marketing machine and various weapons designers are taking a crack at making the old statement "The pen is mightier than the sword" into an actual statement of fact (sort of). No, I'm not talking about pen guns—cool as they are—or even those pens that have a really shitty blade inside; I'm talking about that new kid on the hurting people scene...the **tactical pen.** And before someone bitches about how "A pen cannot be tactical; tactical refers to tactics", shut the hell up, because I'm getting around to tactics...tactical thinking is pretty much the point of this entire chapter, you jackass.

Take the pen in question as an example; at its core it is nothing more than an overbuilt pen, generally made of machined aluminum, steel, titanium or brass. Now sure, some manufactures make theirs look extra flashy, advertising secondary uses to drive up sales; they might not be the best choice (tactically speaking...how many times can I fit "tactics" in here I wonder...). Some are more blunt ended while others are pointier, but that's not different than with any other pen. And that's the whole point, really.

What makes it "tactical" isn't marketing, and it isn't even design so much either, although the strongest ones are obviously better for evil-bashing needs. What makes them tactical is the end goal they'll be used to reach, and your tactics for reaching said goal. Take a blunt one and use it as a kubotan, poking and squishing nerve clusters for inflicting pain, or as a fist-load for the good old fashioned "caveman smash" style of hammerfist bashing fun. Use the pointier versions for stabbing attacks to eyes, neck, and to inflict pain all over the rest of the body. By the way, to live up to the chapter's title, some of the sturdier ones can indeed be driven through a skull. ☺

The point of it all is that by looking at ordinary, everyday objects in a new light, a whole world of previously unseen options for crime-fighting opens up. Never be unarmed wherever you go! Don't put off bashing those thugs' skulls in just because the baseball bat had to stay at home. Just because you cannot transport a child molester to your *Lair of Death* doesn't mean a proper torturing is out of the question. Perhaps the place you've travelled to bans pepper spray... but do they ban "steak spices"? Expand your mind and expand the opportunities for violent adventure any place at any time.

Canes:

What could be more innocuous than a simple cane? As long as there's no sword inside of it, no one gives a shit about some guy walking around with a cane. Bring it to the museum, court, the airport... there's even guys with canes in prison, for fuck's sake! Unless you're wearing a pimp hat and a fur coat while hollering at hoes, a cane is about as low-key as one can get for a crime-bashing implement.

Yes, they really are great for cracking open a skull, disarming a knife-wielding thug or augmenting arm-locks. They'll also help to limp your ass home if things go a tad wrong and injury results, so that's a nice side bonus (I remember that time limping along with a twisted ankle and stab wound to the quadriceps...good times). But not all canes are created equal, so it'll help to know what you're looking for.

1) Canes with sturdy, solid brass handles offer great bashing power in a stylish package, so long as the attachment to the shaft is rock solid; having it go flying off into the night is *very* embarrassing. Look for attachment screws and a shaft which is fitted into a socket in the brass head.

2) Irish Blackthorn and other hardwood root-knob walking sticks make lovely evil-crushing sticks as well. Just make sure to get one with a large root knob; it feels better in the hand while walking, plus adds mass in the right way for cracking bones. Study up on authentic Irish stick-fighting, and bring a touch o' class to the mean streets.

3) **Cane Masters** is a company that produces <u>very</u> sturdy versions of the standard crook-handled cane; offered in hickory, oak, ash, cherry and maple woods. They are definitely aimed at martial arts/defensive use, and certain models offer unique "enhancements" as well...check them out. They also offer instructional videos which teach their style of cane fighting.

4) **TDI** also offers a crook-handle style cane in thick-walled aluminum; very sturdy, but a tad heavy. The extra weight is okay for scum removal purposes though.

The offerings from Cane Masters and TDI all work great with Hapkido cane fighting techniques; actually, Hapkido techniques also work well with standard, cheap crook-handle canes too. The advantages of the aforementioned canes (Cane Masters and TDI) are strength, mass for bashing, and looking cooler while remaining unobtrusive. Other systems of stick-fighting exist as well, so get out there and train!

Steak Spice:

We all know how handy pepper spray can be when out there imposing our iron wills on the criminal scum plaguing society. What you may not know, however, is that the basic concept of blinding agents is not new at all. It is, in fact a *very* old idea, tracing a lineage back to when the first cave-dude grabbed a handful of dirt to throw in his opponent's eyes. Over time the concept became more refined, finding expression in the blinding powder of those legendary agents of silent death, the mysterious ninja.

The ninja (or ninjas...both plural forms are acceptable) developed a special "sand" that could be thrown into their enemies' eyes as a blinding powder. Various recipes were employed, but common ones used sand as a carrier (for distance), along with some form of hot, ground pepper. Sometimes iron filings or glass dust were added for a particularly nasty—and painful—effect. Concoctions of light weight could be blown into the eyes from close range with a hollow tube, like a blowgun.

That doesn't really fit the low-key, everyday objects approach though, does it? Not many folks walk around these days with a pocket full of pepper and glass dust; blow guns aren't common carry items either, even in locales where they're legal to own. So, if one wishes to avoid being arrested as some sort of freak, this handy, modern alternative will do wonders for you; steak spice.

Your own steak spice though, not some pre-made junk off the shelf! The proprietary blend of savoury gastronomic delight is also your perfectly legal justification for carrying it around; you hate the shitty spices they offer at restaurants. You can even eat some in front of the cops if need be.

Simply combine salt as the carrier (tastes better than sand); black pepper; cayenne pepper, and onion powder as well. Mix well and place it in a small container with an easy to flip-up/off lid. To use, simply pop the top and throw it in the eyes of the next thug needing a good beat-down.

As an added bonus, it really does make an awesome steak spice too. ☺

Pencils:

The humble wooden pencil is a fan favourite for shanking folks in prison. Some convicts even prefer them to other shanks because they enjoy the option to break it off in the wound. Most prisons also haven't banned pencils, despite having the harshest anti-weapon laws on the planet. So why not take a tip from crime and use that tip to stab it in the eye?

From the schoolyard to the prison-yard, pencils are an innocuous object permitted due to legitimate uses. Before the pressurized "space pen" cartridges were developed, regular pencils were used to write upside down and in space. No one will think it odd that there are some pencils in your backpack (or purse, for female undercover heroines).

To use, simply stab the soft spots of the human body; eyes, throat, and any exposed fleshy areas. Mechanical pencils are plenty stabby also, and have more strength to aid in penetration. They lack the option to bust it off in the wound though, robbing you of the entertainment value inherent to watching a scummy crook squirm as the wooden shard pokes internal body parts with every motion.

Scissors:

Wouldn't it be great to have sturdy stabbing capability just about anywhere you go, even by air? How about having something with you to cut stuff despite having left the knife at home? Did you know you can bring pointy scissors on an airplane in carry-on luggage as long as the blade is less than 4 inches in length?

Yep, that's right; scissors can even be taken on airplanes! They also have the same stabbing power as a push-dagger (illegal just about everywhere, especially for carry); you can punch straight through a skull with those babies as long as the point is acute and you didn't purchase cheap junk. Although they don't have the same "cool factor" as a stylish push-dagger, the criminal whose skull they just pierced won't say anything...because he'll be dead.

Magazines:

What do you do when some fuck-face sneaks a carbon fiber knife onto the plane and gets big-minded ideas about going all jihad on everyone's ass? Simple; armour and weapon-up with magazines (and some tape...tape would be handy). Taping a medium thickness magazine on each forearm provides makeshift vambraces with good slash and stab resistance. Then just tightly roll up a magazine; held closed with some tape it makes a very study baton for jabbing attacks. Hitting with the butt end of it with hammerfist strikes will produce some very rewarding blunt attack damage.

Large Bandanas and Shemaghs:

Just because you're going low key doesn't mean a lack of need for identity protection. When leaping into action, the benefits as far as fun is concerned are worth thinking of as well. Masks are just plain fun, and make the superhero lifestyle really "pop" for some reason or other; as discussed previously, the anonymity aspect can really aid in getting the fuck out of there afterward.

So try carrying a large bandana or shemagh with you! In the bottom of a bag it's just a piece of cloth; could be a scarf; could be carried as an emergency sling (works for that too); either one can also make a useful towel for cleaning spills. The point being that it's not the same thing as being found with a balaclava in your gym bag...far less suspicion arousing.

Plus you can always do the old "pool ball in a bandana" trick with it; substitute a can of cola in your bag instead of a pool ball, and let the bashing fun commence!

Hand Sanitizer, Vaseline and Napkins:

Everyone knows about the value of alcohol-based hand sanitizer for killing all those nasty germs out there. Napkins make it easy to wipe the hands dry quicker (getting rid of dirt/grease too; alcohol makes a good solvent), and allows for cleaning tape residue gunk off of knives, as well as other things of that nature. Vaseline helps restore moisture balance to skin after using all that nasty alcohol; that's why it forms the basis for many hand lotions. You just prefer the pure thing with no additives. Available in a handy range of container sizes, both are very easy to carry around with you. They also make good fire-starters...and that's where we enter the story.

You see, the jellied alcohol nature of it gives a *very slight* napalm-like effect which is good for getting fires going in survival situations. This also translates into being a good accelerant for assisting in getting an evidence destroying blaze going. Vaseline rubbed on a napkin or into the fabric of a couch will work just as well, possibly better; it's a petroleum product...unleash the fury of dead dinosaurs upon the abode of dead criminals.

Multi-tools and Butane Torch Lighters = Torture on the Go:

The multi-tool—be it in the form of a Swiss Army Knife or Leatherman—has become a widely carried and highly useful implement. The multitude of handy tools makes any job easier, and most folks don't even consider it a knife, even when it has locking blades. With the addition of pliers (starting with the Leatherman but later incorporated in some Swiss Army Knives as well) simply adding to the perception of utility first, weapon almost never.

Butane torch (or windproof) lighters are another thing everyone should have on them anyway. Whether lost in the woods or simply lighting a cigarette for a damsel in distress, the capacity to create fire on demand is what separates us from the animals. Fire and the sharp edge; they're pretty much our two oldest and most important tools as human beings.

They'll also work very well for all your torture needs while out and about. Sometimes you just can't transport degenerates back to the *Lair of Death*, whether because of family, financial constraints (still amassing the cash for land and building supplies), or any of a wide range of issues which just pop up. Or how about when the freak lets it slip that there's a buried crate of cheerleaders about to suffocate if not promptly rescued? You don't have time to fuck around playing mind games **or** bother with transportation time; answers must be had <u>now</u>.

But that's no problem, because you have a butane torch lighter and a Leatherman; soon you'll have the requisite answers. Simply drag him off to the nearest abandoned building, and start burning bits away. Torch an eyeball; burn out an ear (leave one for hearing questions though!); burning the palm of the hand gets results...you get the picture.

163

The Leatherman with pliers is pretty self-explanatory; grip bits of anatomy and crush, pull or tear. The other tools like the saw, can opener and other things will get results too. Just experiment and learn on the go; there's almost no wrong way to do it.

Although there are other everyday items which will serve your heroic needs, they needn't all be listed. This sampling is sufficient to get the mental gears grinding in the correct direction to keep the Justice Rampage going full-swing for years, no matter what legal restrictions may be placed in your path.

But while you're rampaging, what words will burst forth from your lips? What mighty shout will rob the criminals of their resolve to fight back, putting them at an immediate disadvantage whenever you appear? Well, you'd best put your best thinking mask on and pop a few ephedrine, because it's time to find out! It's time to discover your battle-cry.

{CHAPTER 25} MAKE THEM PISS THEIR PANTS: BATTLE-CRY ESSENTIALS

"Excuse me, but could you please stop committing crime now?"

That is not what you want in a battle-cry. Meek is weak; you want strong, bold and possibly confusing. Something like The Tick's mighty yell of *"Spoon!"* as he leaps into battle; evildoers just don't know what the fuck is going on in time to avoid being clobbered all to hell. Over time the criminal bastards came to know that this was the cry of Justice coming to punch them in the face, but even before that it had a powerfully confusing effect. You can capture this with a cry of your own such as *"Save the whales!"* as battle is met; chop them to quivering piles of meat using the Machete of Decency, savouring the stupid look on their faces.

Disgust Based Approach: Perhaps you're going for the shock value of pure disgust...this is also acceptable. Throw them off with a mighty shout of *"I'll rape your face!"* or *"I shit my pants!"* Likewise, lustily call out in a booming voice *"I fuck goats!"* and reap the benefits as they freeze in momentarily shock...which is the entire point of it all. Gain the upper hand by inducing their disgust reaction; people cannot process simultaneous mental stimuli very well for the most part.

Name Based Approach: The name based approach is always popular as well; if you have an inspiring, terrorizing—or just plain cool—name, this approach may be appealing. Simply announce your heroic identity to the world, and then leap into action! *"You face Black Death, Victorious Conqueror of Evil!"* Not bad, not bad at all. Or combine your name with some sort of situational observation: *"You've done the crime, now you must face Brutal Justice!"* So if you love your name and enjoy posing in the mirror while wearing your sexy mask and body armour, this is your option of choice. Tell the world *exactly* how you are! <u>*Proclaim*</u> your greatness, shouting it in the faces of those idiotic enough to challenge your might.

The "Insane Gibberish" Approach: This is aimed at blurting out the sorts of words and phrases which confuse the fuck out of people. The example of ***"Spoon!"*** was used earlier, and I'll use it again because it's a great example of what you're trying for. You want something simple and forceful to say, something that provides the same shouting out power as *"Shit!"* and *"Fuck!"*...and ***"Spoon!"*** truly captures it. Try it with common words, till you find a few that really resonate for you. It could be ***"Sandwich!"*** or ***"Snapple!"*** even; it's for you to find out, not me or anyone else.

Or simply blurt the very first words that enter consciousness, so that what is said is a surprise even to you, pretty much. Unlock the doors to the subconscious mind; you may just find the unlocking of other abilities as well.

The Fear-Inducing Approach: You're gonna terrify those slimy bastards; they'll quake in their boots before they die, fearing you more than Satan himself (by the way, **<u>Fuck you Satan!</u>** What a total dick)...am I forgetting anything?

Probably not, because that's what the whole fear-inducing approach is all about; pure psychological manipulation. Just look at Batman's whole approach; he applied psychology to the whole thing and crafted an image specifically designed to spread fear in his target audience. It is a pretty good fictional model for what you intend.

It's harder for you in the real world though, because actual muggers and rapists don't have scripted reactions to your actions. Some will drop in fear from a hard glance, but others are hardened criminals who just won't care what you say at all...but *you* may still benefit. By attempting to induce fear in another individual, you can transfer any you may have (assuming you have any, that is ☺) as well as insulate yourself from developing any, even if things go wrong.

And if you can't scare him with your words, then scare him with his own intestines, pulled from the gaping wound in his abdomen!

That's pretty much the basics of it all. As before, you are encouraged to engage your lateral thinking skills and blend from all the categories you wish. The main thing is that it *pumps you up for battle*; the actual destruction of evil is still the goal as always, so use all possible tools to root it out.

But where do you find the crime, and how? Can it really be as easy as walking down random alleys and encountering opportunities for violent adventure? (Spoiler alert: it usually ain't). Why are the cops still managing to find more crime to arrest than you...is it sheer numbers? Or do they maybe have a strategy, a crime-fighting strategy...

{CHAPTER 26} SAMPLE CRIME-FIGHTING STRATEGIES

Now obviously the methods you employ as a violent vigilante operating outside the protective aegis of the law will tend to be rather different than those used by police forces in civilized countries (although you may wish to check out some of the things Third World security forces do for some truly brutal ideas). Many of the actual strategies to locate crime can actually be adopted from the cops and used to brutal effect in our own crime-destroying missions; there is no need to reinvent the wheel.

You see, the cops actually do a decent job many times of finding the scum of society. Their lack of impact on crime comes from the legal red tape that binds their hands and cuts them out of the punishment business. In addition, the courts take a bloody long, money wasting time deciding what to do with the accused afterward, and often release them back upon society. So cut the cops some slack; they are often doing the best job possible with the tools society puts in their hands. Take the good ideas and simply add a heaping helping of extreme brutality.

Patrolling ("Patrol, Patrol, You *Must* Learn Patrol!"):

This is the first thing any hero does as soon as the decision is made to head out into the night in search of evil and adventure. It is also the reason many heroes don't hold the course...because it can be boring at times. Perhaps the issue is that people might be doing it wrong; or perhaps the boredom of it all is why so many cops can be found in donut shops or napping in patrol cars. Let's look a little closer.

Random and Set Route Patrols: This is the mainstay of traditional police work, and does actually have a measurable crime-reduction effect. The officer sets out on foot or in a vehicle, and simply patrols around an area. In most cases there is a certain district to be patrolled, and the routes can either be set by the cop (or command), or entirely random. Even set routes tend to be patrolled at random times in order to avoid criminals figuring out when the best time to commit crimes is; truly random ones add an extra level of unpredictability. When going full random, care must be taken to hit all necessary patrol points, as they can be missed through absent-mindedness.

The *Random Encounters* hero type naturally follows this methodology, and has no issue with boredom when doing so (or else they would have chosen a different path). Other hero types will often end up doing this at times too; however, they'll often end up bored as beat cops, and find themselves drinking coffee in a late-night diner far more often than being engaged in glorious combat. Perhaps a tweak on the basic concept could help...

"Hotspot" Policing...Maximize Patrol Effectiveness: Why waste time patrolling where the crime isn't happening? That's the question many police forces have asked, and it's one you'll ask yourself too after the 27th patrol with no incidents to report. The answer is simple enough though, and obvious after a little thought; search the crime statistics and find out where the fucking crime is actually going down.

Police use various computer software and analysis tactics to sift through a mountain of crime stats; you don't have an entire crime-fighting staff (probably...maybe you do) to allocate such jobs to. The good news is that interactive crime maps make it possible to figure out overall trends on the cheap (they're free) in order to maximize your chances of happening across a crime in progress. Many of the online resources allow for setting parameters such as crime categories to be displayed, as well as specifying the time-frame to be searched. Just set it up and gaze at the pretty little crime flags which pop up, showing a smorgasbord of crime; as I write this, the map shows where I should be heading next...I can feel the pulse-pounding adrenaline surge of combat coming on already!

Be warned, however, that even when one heads into the best areas for violent fun, crime remains random and sporadic (I know, it's a bummer at times). Perhaps you'll feel better after stabbing a child molester or two; if so, try the next strategy.

Internet Luring:

The internet has changed everything, including how we track down awesome gear options, fancy clothes, and even how people meet to start relationships. As with anything good though, there's also a darker side; child molesters use the power of the Web to attempt the initiation of "relationships" with young children and pre-teens. The increased ability to communicate over large distances combined with an ability to maintain anonymity has seen skyrocketing predation on children, the most vulnerable members of society. The Digital Age is also the downfall of those sick, sick perverts...

You see, the capacity for anonymous communication they rely on to ensnare victims is a double-edged sword, and we can chop them down with it! The cops have personnel dedicating to luring these degenerate fuckers into coming to a spot where they can be arrested. The officer poses online as a child of the appropriate age... the hard part is using language (spelling, grammar, vocabulary) which is convincingly like someone of the supposed age would use. A game of "internet fishing" commences, and if the pedophile bastard is lured effectively, a meeting place and time is arranged.

You can do the very same thing. Set up a meeting—a cheap motel is a favourite—and get to work on that scum with a crowbar and some pliers. Shitty apartments with no leases, low rent and "cash only" policies are another great locale for such operations. The great thing is that you can just sit back and enjoy a nice cup of coffee along with a roast beef sandwich while waiting for the fun to commence.

This sort of ploy works best for the pedophile type of criminal scum, although it can also be modified for other types of sting operations; why not arrange a meeting with someone posting under the "Casual Encounters" section? Often it becomes known that a certain profile picture is being used to advertise for gay sex or prostitution, but then a guy comes along to beat, rob or sometimes rape the person who responded. The cops often don't get contacted because the victim feels shame, and won't advertise what happened...at least to the authorities. They often <u>will</u> warn other prospective respondents through message boards. The point is to open up your "internet ears" and listen for the Justice opportunities patiently awaiting a hero such as yourself.

I set up a meeting with this scummy pedophile via the Internet. Said I was a 14 year old boy that would meet him under this bridge after school. Little did he know that I would be there instead, along with my apprentice. I approach silently from behind, and grab him by the neck (my apprentice lurks off to the side...)

I begin the application of Justice by stepping alongside the pervert, keeping a firm grasp of his neck (note the footwork...as I keep telling my apprentice, footwork is paramount!)

My leg goes ahead of his; the next step ends with...

...his face getting slammed into the ground!

The knife is poised to deliver the fatal blow.

That should do the trick.

This is a good learning experience for my apprentice, so I beckon him over.

Well done! That sword thrust would have been fatal all on its own. And I didn't even have to tell him where to place the strike... they grow up so fast, don't they?

Stakeouts:

Sometimes the cops get a tip of something to go down at a certain time; sometimes they simply need more info on a particular group or scummy individual. Either way it adds up to time for yet another crime-fighting strategy...the stakeout. If you thought endless patrols were boring, just wait till you're sitting in a cramped car for hours on end, or the back of a stuffy van; it can get dull, too hot or too cold, and your back will scream obscenities at you.

You'll end up doing stakeouts when trying to determine the criminal status of certain locations (suspected drug houses and such), as well as the best times to strike. Method of stakeout might be the old classic of sitting in a car or the back of a van fitted with surveillance equipment, but could also go in different directions. Perhaps a handy coffee shop is within view of the crack-house, or a bus stop where the fucking bus only comes once an hour (inconvenient for travel; convenient for short stakeouts). Perhaps dress as an alcoholic bum and lay in the trash of a convenient alley...it has been done before to good effect.

Of course, with technology commonly available today, there is no reason for you to even be present. Hunters use those hunting cameras with video recording and many, many hours of storage capacity. You are a hunter of criminals, so why not do the same; simply place a hunting camera in a handy spot with good visibility and let it do all the boring stuff! They aren't too hard to hide either, certainly easier than concealing an entire human. Then, when enough time has passed in your opinion, go collect it—or them—and review the footage. If instant action is required, use a camera that transmits the video stream in addition to recording; then sit in a nearby area monitoring it on a laptop or smart phone. Repurpose that ubiquitous technology to a more noble usage.

Bait Patrol (Recruit a Weakling to the Cause...):

As has been noted by various heroes, they ran out there into the night with a mask on, thinking they were really going to make a difference. Criminals of the sort targeted did not cooperate, however; the ones who remain in operation have gotten pretty good at not getting caught, and thus do not usually operate out in the open. So you have to give them a little bait...

Police forces use this tactic all the time; prostitution stings and setting up drug buys with undercover agents are the most common of these. They ride the fine line of entrapment in a legal sense, but the tactic keeps getting use because it just plain <u>works</u>. You should do the same, except leave the prostitutes alone; they aren't a high impact criminal group, and are often victims of more nefarious evildoers themselves. Let the police deal with chasing them out of "nice" neighbourhoods.

You're going to be trolling for muggers and rapists mainly, as those are the street-level thugs best lured out for disposal by this ploy. You *could* make the attempt to use yourself as bait; dress up in your flashiest clothes, and put on lots of extra expensive jewellery. Like I said, you *could* try this...but if you're male and have been keeping up with your steroids, nutrition and exercise regimen, it'll be awfully difficult to portray the correct level of helpless vulnerability required to entice the average mugger. Most rapists won't try victimizing a huge, muscular man either, which certainly takes the bait role out of your hands. So, what should a physically potent, violent vigilante superhero do then?

Answer: Recruit a weakling. ☺ I know that this brings risks along with benefits (discussed under the section on <u>super-teams</u>), but if you want to drive up the Justice numbers, there's really no better way when targeting street-rat savages. So find someone who is trustworthy but decidedly <u>not</u> physically formidable. It may be possible to maintain a veil of anonymity even; keep them from ever knowing your secret identity...after all, they just have to be bait in order to bring out the slime. Either way though, you must be in the immediate vicinity in order to swoop in and save the day, so some means of communication like a Bluetooth earpiece or 2-way radio should be used.

Working Your Way up the Criminal Food Chain:

The cops almost never get the head of a Mafia family in custody right off the bat (or ever, for that matter); they have to start lower on the criminal food chain and work their way to the top-level predators. So they arrest some low-level drug dealers, and interrogate them in hopes of getting info on those who really control the action. Threats of prison time are made, or sometimes plea bargain deals to reduce or avoid serving time altogether are put forth. And it works...sort of... some of the time. The problem the police face involves in part the fact that the low-level thugs know that the penalty for snitching can be **far worse** than any amount of prison time; also, the cops can't employ torture techniques in order to encourage cooperation.

This is not a problem you share, however, especially if you've gone ahead and built your custom *Lair of Death* as described in a previous chapter. It's amazing the amount of cooperation one can gain with the assistance of a fully stocked torture chamber. ☺ You must be careful of one phenomenon though; false confessions. The thing of it is that people will say <u>anything</u> in order to stop a certain level of pain. Justice will not come by inaccurate targeting; the correct scum must be destroyed, not some innocent schlub thrown under the bus by a screaming pedophile attempting to end the torment. So be careful to *avoid asking leading questions*...let the truth pour out freely along with the blood, and avoid making those embarrassing rookie interrogation mistakes.

Let Your Subconscious Mind be the Guide:

Okay, this one isn't used by cops, or at least is never admitted to (although some do occasionally use psychics on tough cases when all else fails). The idea is that your conscious mind isn't always the best guide to things; the subconscious notices and retains information that flies right past normal cognition. You may have noticed this with dreams, and indeed some of the toughest problems in science have been solved through the power of the subconscious manifesting during dreamtime; Kekulé's dream of the Ouroboros unlocked the ring structure of Benzene, for fuck's sake! So what can you do to unlock such insight for superhero purposes?

The answer is to introduce a random element into the mix; it's time to consult the oracle. Or perhaps the term should be oracles, for there are many. The Norse runes; dowsing with a pendulum; throwing the bones or reading tarot cards...it's all the same idea. By introducing such randomizers into the solution seeking process, it is possible to bypass the linearly logical processes of normal, waking consciousness. In the random patterns and ambiguous signs, the subconscious is free to superimpose the patterns it sees, thus bringing things into a different focus.

So go unleash the power of your subconscious mind upon crime!

Well, it's been a long crazy ride, but you're now pretty much ready to hit the streets and wipe the criminal slime clean off the planet. Obviously there will be some mistakes made along the way—nothing worthwhile is totally easy—but by applying the lessons contained within this handy guidebook, you'll be assured of great success in your Brutal Crusade of Justice. The life-path being embarked upon will bring endless adventure and huge levels of self-actualization; the core of your being will be free to develop beyond what most mortals can even dream of.

But before bidding you adieu, I'll share the wisdom from others who have walked this path before. Drink it all in, and gain the benefit from sampling a multitude of perspectives; for while we all walk the spiral path of Justice and Glory, we remain fiercely individual, with myriad viewpoints and ways of viewing this amazing thing we call existence.

{CHAPTER 27} INSPIRATIONAL STORIES AND MOTIVATIONAL THOUGHTS: WISDOM FROM EXPERIENCE

You're jumping off into an amazing life filled with constant adventure; there's always something new to do, places to explore, crimes to be thwarted and damsels to rescue. Training and learning new skills of <u>all</u> sorts will occupy an entire lifetime's worth of study, but you'll constantly grow better, stronger, smarter and more resolute. I salute you for your commitment.

Some things only become apparent with the passage of time, and the accumulation of those observations is the basis for what we call <u>wisdom</u>. Hear what the heroes of the past and present have to say in the way of inspirational accounts of things done along the way, and motivational thoughts which serve to keep heroics fresh and adventurous, the way it should be.

- "I will <u>not</u> settle for the mediocre existence; I crave adventure, new horizons and new vistas to experience. If I live 100 thousand years there will still be new things to do, places to see, evils to be brutally fought. The lack of imagination I see amongst the masses is a curse I do not share in." {*Iron Justice*, October 5, 2011}
- The life of a superhero is an odd sort of thing. One day you're battling high level villains...the next day is spent in a shack on stakeout duty.
- The first step to being Superhuman is refusing to accept limitations.
- "Let's suppose for a moment that you're ready to go full vigilante; good for you! More people need to get on board the harsh Justice train. As one of the proud few who possess the guts to stomp the foul scum into a sticky paste, a whole

world of adventure awaits, especially once you expand the range of crimes which merit a savage beating. People who litter can be locked in rancid dumpsters. Those fucking jerks who blare their shitty cellphones like a boom-box sure are annoying, am I right? Of course I am, so why not bash their teeth down their stupid throats with their own goddamned phone?

Do you see the pattern here? Don't just be vicious, be ironic! Filthy asshole didn't wash his hands after taking a dump? Wash his <u>eyes</u> with a generous amount of hand sanitizer. Child molesters should in turn be molested...by horny goats. Get creative with it. ☺ " {*Golden Panda*, June 27, 2004}

- It ain't about the size of the criminal in the fight; it's about the size of the knife in his neck.
- "I like going out there and fighting crime as a civilian, with no real legal authority to back me up. Fuck yeah!!!" {*Sloth Fist, Violent Lover of Justice*, May 5, 1985}
- Take your weirdness outdoors.
- Terrorism must be answered with Justice!
- Badass is beating someone up to the tune of their own music.
- <u>Remember</u>: If you're walking down the street and zero crime is occurring, it's because <u>you're</u> there. The cops take credit for crime prevention due to mere presence all the time...so can you.
- "So then the dumbass goes running away from me, and ends up getting run over by a drunk driver. He died and the moron driver went to prison; win-win situation, oh yeah. Funniest fucking thing I saw all year." {*Night Being, Dangerous Destroyer*, September 19, 2002}
- It takes all types to make the world go round...but some people's purpose in life is for punching practice.

Day 3406

The yacht bobs temptingly in the waters comprising the Gulf of Oman. A jewel of gaudy opulence, it ill fits in with this impoverished part of the world. A rich man's folly intended to attract envious intent from all who gaze upon her. In other words, a target...all it needs is for a predator to sight it.

Lo, upon the horizon, what is this? Is it, can it be...oh fuck, it is! Pirates!! Modern day pirates, with a rusty skiff instead of a splintery, leaky and creaky wooden sailing vessel of yore. At least it leaks; that is a nice nod to tradition.

Sweaty, poorly attired bony men thrust surplus AK-47 rifles and RPG launchers in the air, pumping them energetically as if entreating the gods to smile upon their villainous enterprise. Their voices cry out into the humid air, howling a wordless, timeless raiding song, ancient before man could fully comprehend the concepts encoded therein. Yet, primal as it is, <u>powerful as it is</u>, the distance between predator and prey is too great to be sonically breached.

As the distance decreases, figures on the yacht come into focus for the pirates. Running back and forth along the railing, they frantically wave their arms and cry out "Help!" and "Go away, leave us alone!" Grins spread across the faces of the sweaty scum, as anticipation of another easy hijacking builds; the rewards are just as sweet, and risk or hard work is not required.

Something seems a tad off though; one does not remain a Somalian pirate for long without developing some instincts...still, that loot won't bring itself ashore, so the skiff continues its approach. As boarding distance approaches, details begin to resolve into greater focus... why do the exact same pleas seem on a loop...why is there tape on the passenger's mouths...why are their hands covered with taped on mitts...are they chained to the railing, just sliding along the rail as they run...Oh. Fuck.

The pirates' eyes widen, and tears roll down the cheeks of those chained to the yacht...

I smile. ☺

Click.

*An almighty **"Boom!"** announces the birth of a fireball which reaches for the heavens. A shockwave races across the water and debris flies in all directions. I put the binoculars down and feel a sense of satisfaction suffuse my soul. It's amazing the sheer devastation a couple dozen pounds of C4 and a remote detonator can wreak. And I even found a good use for those Egyptian child sex-slave peddlers I captured a few days back; every trap needs bait.*

This calls for a fine cigar.

Damn I'm good. **{Stabman, date unspecified}**

- I can change your facts. Your truth holds no boundaries for me.
- When action is needed, doubts are irrelevant.
- "I stalk through the night, unobtrusively relentless, with vengeance in my heart and pockets full of death. A lethal variant on the Santa Claus archetype, those deemed evil receive a heaping helping of fatal Justice!" {*Death Owl*, August 11, 1982}
- Brutality is the key to victory. Ill-timed kindness is fatal, generally to the one being kind.
- Fear is wasted energy. Paranoia hands victory to the enemy.
- When life hands you lemons, find the closest criminal scum and *cram* those lemons down their evil throat, choking the life from their corrupt body with the fruit of Justice!
- I put on my mask to scare the fear away.
- Controlled brutality is one path to Justice.
- Armoured up, the combat drugs are kicking in, and I have all the evildoers heavily out-clamped. ☺
- You know, it's weird but when I see a group of 5 to 6 guys, I want to jump <u>them</u>. Fear is not an option.
- It is only by adventuring throughout the world that one can stumble across the exciting danger.
- Attitude trumps equipment.
- I fear not the danger, for I <u>am</u> the danger.
- You can't be right about anything without being wrong a lot of times too.

- We in the hero business don't have the luxury of apathy. The City cries out for a protector, and we must man-up, suit-up and venture forth regardless of adversity.
- I am 100 percent immortality compatible.
- "It's like football, only the goal is Justice!" {Canadian Justice, May 22, 2014}
- Heroics requires the willingness to say "Fuck you!" to the odds.
- I need to run on the rooftops, to stalk through alleys and jump off of buildings. The call of adventure beckons through the hazy gloom of normalcy, and I must harken to the call.
- **"Scars show where we've been, but don't dictate where we're going." {The Destroyer, February 3, 2014}**

**All unattributed motivational thoughts were submitted by heroes who have for one reason or another decided to remain anonymous. **

RECOMMENDED READING

No single book—not even this one—can hope to be fully comprehensive. Human knowledge is very diverse, and in that very diversity lays strength, as well as opportunity. Therefore, I shall share with you a list of books which have been very useful in walking the heroic path, providing examples of what to do, as well as what pitfalls to avoid.

Knife Fighting:

- **Knife Fighting, Knife Throwing For Combat,** Michael D. Echanis (author)
  This book will provide some simple techniques that work well, plus demonstrate a whole bunch of flowing, spinning nonsense to avoid like the plague. A classic text on the topic; just use your brain.
- **Knife Fighting Encyclopedia: Volume 1: The Foundation**, W. Hock Hochheim (author)
  A great book which lays out the fundamentals. Solid information.
- **Knife/Counter-Knife Combatives,** W. Hock Hochheim (author)
  A revamped version of the Encyclopedia, this goes past it to supercharge your skills development. Full of great info and training tips, along with real-life examples.
- **Knife Fighting: A Practical Course**, Michael D. Janich (author)
  A quick to learn system which emphasizes simple concepts and effective techniques. Get ready to slash crime apart in a hurry!
- **Contemporary Knife Targeting: Modern Science vs. W.E. Faibairn's Timetable of Death**, Michael D. Janich and Christopher Grosz (authors)
  Uses modern science in the form of medical studies to see where the classic timetable of where to cut people to bleed

them out efficiently got it right, as well as when it got things wrong. Also includes some techniques to stop attackers in a hurry.

- **Put 'Em Down, Take 'Em Out! Knife Fighting Techniques from Folsom Prison**, Don Pentecost (author)
  This rather slim book deals with how to shank people in prison. It lays out the basic methodology, and shows techniques. The form emphasizes pure aggression and brutal, "sewing machine" stabbing attacks. Learn how your enemies fight; take what works, and figure out how to defeat the evil bastards.

- **Master of the Blade: Secrets of the Deadly Art of Knife Fighting**, Richard Ryan (author)
  One of the most entertaining books on the subject; it also delivers the goods. Although the author is rather arrogant in his opinion regarding his amazingness, he does back up all claims with well thought out reasoning and examples. Another very comprehensive book that provides a great base from which to build.

- **Combat Knife Throwing: A New Approach to Knife Throwing and Knife Fighting**, Ralph Thorn (author)
  The title pretty much says it all. The author shows you how to select, modify and use throwing knives in a manner which could possibly work in a combative situation. Might as well learn how to throw knives for the off chance that it comes into play on some mission along the way.

- **Karambit: Exotic Weapon of the Indonesian Archipelago**, Steve Tarani (author)
  Learn everything you ever wanted to know (and then some) about this snazzy little hook bladed knife. By the end of it, you'll know if karambits are for you or not.

Martial Arts:

- **The Wing Chun Compendium**, Wayne Belonoha (author)
  You're gonna learn Wing Chun! Seriously, this book is fucking huge...going from history to pressure points with everything in between as well. If you ever thought about adding Wing Chun tactics to your tool kit, this'll do for sure.

- **English Martial Arts**, Terry Brown (author)
  Learn all about English martial arts history, as well as getting a primer on how to kick some serious ass with old-timey weaponry.

- **The Martial Arts of Ancient Greece: Modern Fighting Techniques from the Age of Alexander**, Kostas Dervanis and Nektarios Lykiardopoulos (authors)
  Ever wanted to learn how a Greek from the Time of Legend would pull someone's arm off? Read this book and soon you'll be twisting limbs apart like Hercules with a hangover! Tons of historical stuff too.

- **Tao of Jeet Kune Do**, Bruce Lee (author)
  Gain the martial insight of a truly legendary fighter. Lots of observations, philosophy and tactics that will serve you well.

- **Best Judo**, Isao Inokuma and Nobuyuki Sato (authors)
  So much Judo...grappling overload...brain going to explode! Yep, this book is jam-packed with Judo. Get ready to throw criminals through plate glass windows and off of tall buildings. ☺

- **Mas Oyama's Classic Karate**, Tomoko Murakami and Jeffrey Cousminer (translators)
  Mas Oyama was a true badass; killed bulls with his bare hands, and punched trees till they died. Get on board with how the one they called Godhand trained and fought.

- **The Straight Lead: The Core of Bruce Lee's Jun Fan Jeet Kune Do**, Teri Tom (author)
  With an entire book dedicated to performing a single punch— with a few minor variations—you're going to go more in depth than you ever thought possible. Learn just how much there is to throwing a truly effective punch.

Guns and Stuff:

- **Workbench Silencers: The Art of Improvised Designs**, George M. Hollenback (author)
  Need to get rid of that annoying "Bang!" sound your gun keeps making? Fear not, for this book shows how to get around that little problem.

- **The Shotgun in Combat**, Tony Lesce (author)
  With everything from penetration tests to tactics, and even how to properly club people without breaking your gun, this resource will get you set to go out and shoot thugs with a shotgun in all seasons.
- **Expedient Homemade Firearms: The 9mm Submachine Gun**, P.A. Luty (author)
  Learn how to make a 9mm submachine gun out of commonly available parts and simple hand tools! You know you're gonna need a submachine gun at some point along the way; why not add pride of craftsmanship to the mix as well?
- **The Do-It-Yourself Gunpowder Cookbook**, Don McLean (author)
  What good is a gun without gunpowder? Although this book is rather slim, it's jam-packed with more than you ever needed to know about manufacturing gunpowder; it even tells you how to mine or make the components for it! Guns, bombs or whatever your gunpowder needs may be, you need to get this book.
- **Zips, Pipes, and Pens: Arsenal of Improvised Weapons**, J. David Truby (author)
  There's some truly James Bond shit in here, and though it doesn't exactly give detailed manufacturing plans, you'll figure it out easily enough. Pen guns, lighter guns, cane guns…even machineguns made in remote jungle workshops. A main premise of the book is that with ammo, you can improvise a gun to fire it; with a gun, you can improvise ammo to fit it. Hmmm, why not do both…

Generalized Fighting:

- **Fighting the Pain Resistant Attacker: fighting drunks, dopers, the deranged and others who tolerate pain**, Loren W. Christensen (author)
  Find out how to effectively smash those fuckers who just don't feel pain like a normal human. A pretty comprehensive treatment of the subject.

- **FTW Self Defense**, C.R. Jahn (author)
  This book covers snazzy topics such as improvised weapons, gun selection, and a very bare-bones method of killing with knives. Very valuable for its breakdown of the various sub-categories of scum which infest our world; learn the difference between sleazebags, punks, freaks and others, as well as how best to deal with them. Very well written...you'll enjoy it.
- **Surviving Armed Assaults: A Martial Artist's Guide to Weapons, Street Violence, & Countervailing Force**, Lawrence A. Kane (author)
  Although aimed at self-defense rather than brutally imposing Justice, it will still give you all the info you need about how to deal with a wide range of weapons threats in a multitude of situations.
- **Krav Maga: How to Defend Yourself Against Armed Attacks**, Imi Sde-Or and Eyal Yanilov (authors)
  Learn how to defend against attacks from people armed with knives, guns, sticks, and even goddamned grenades! A must for all who go out doing what we do.
- **Cold Steel: Technique of Close Combat**, John Styers (author)
  Learn to fight like a Marine. Whether you're unarmed, holding a knife, club or even a bayonet, this book will get you up to combat effectiveness with simple and direct techniques.

Dim-Mak (Death-Touch):

- **Death Touch: The Science Behind the Legend of Dim-Mak**, Michael Kelly, D.O. (author)
  This book is interesting in that it actually explores the physical basis for what dim-mak is really doing. Learn a butt-load more about the nervous system than you probably currently do.
- **Dim-Mak: Death-Point Striking**, Erle Montaigue (author)
  This is one of his earlier books, and he goes quite in-depth as to how to strike and grip these targets. You should probably read it first actually, and then go on to the rest.

- **The Encyclopedia of Dim-Mak: The Main Meridians,** Erle Montaigue and Wally Simpson (authors)
  An enormous book covering an immense number of pressure point pressing and striking targets. Pick the ones you can corroborate with medical science and fight footage, and go to town!
- **The Encyclopedia of Dim-Mak: The Extra Meridians, Points, and more**, Erle Montaigue and Wally Simpson (authors)
  Here's the rest of the targets that wouldn't fit into the first gigantic book.

Stick Fighting:

- **Stickfighting: A Practical Guide for Self-Protection**, Evan S. Baltazzi (author)
  Learn how to fight with a stick about the length of a cane. Not the end-all-be-all book on the subject, but it does give a lot of good info you can use right away.
- **Stick Fighting: techniques of self-defense**, Masaaki Hatsumi and Quintin Chambers (authors)
  Add the ancient Japanese art of stick fighting to your arsenal. It covers techniques for use with a wide range in size of sticks, from pen-sized pocket-sticks all the way up to full staffs. Very heavily grappling based; learn how to twist criminals into a pretzel with nothing more than a simple stick.

Swordsmanship:

- **English Swordsmanship: The True Fight of George Silver, Vol. 1**, Stephen Hand (author)
  His system transitions from the Medieval style into the Renaissance, blending into a beautiful method of dismembering your adversary. Get all stylish with your machete next time you're facing a group of scum-rot savages deserving of death!

- **Medieval Swordsmanship: Illustrated Methods and Techniques**, John Clements (author)
  If one replaces the armour with a modern bullet-resistant version, and substitutes a ballistic shield in place of a wooden one, it is possible to truly go Medieval on some scum. Start kickin it old-school...really old-school.
- **Medieval Combat: A Fifteenth-Century Manual of Swordfighting and Close-Quarter Combat**, Hans Talhoffer (author) and Mark Rector (translator and editor)
  Holy shit, there is some truly crazy stuff in here! Whether you're using a pool cue in a bar-room brawl or facing a loony who's wielding a sword, you'll find inspiration for success within these pages.

Getting into the Proper Vigilante Mindset:

- **Knights of Darkness: Secrets of the World's Deadliest Night Fighters**, Dr. Haha Lung (author)
  You'll feel inspired to run off into the night in search of forbidden adventure! Full of a mix of both good and questionable information, it is valuable nonetheless for sheer motivational effectiveness.
- **Stabman: Diary of a Superhero/Psycho**, Mark Sewell (author)
  No other book will take you into the vigilante mindset as well as this does. From internal motivations to tactics and mistakes made along the way, you'll get the full picture. Be inspired to new heights of bold adventuring. Be inspired to become...a superhero! Warning: Not recommended for timid readers.
- **Subway Survival! The Art Of Self-Defense On American Public Transit Facilities**, Bradley J. Steiner (author)
  This book from 1980 is chock-full of great vigilante thinking. From distrust of "the system" to constant willingness for insane levels of overkill, it has it all. Step into the land of violence, and pull up a seat for the freak-show.

- **<u>Becoming Batman: The Possibility of a Superhero</u>**, E. Paul Zehr (author)

  This is one of the oddest books in that it actually sets out to figure out what it would take to become and remain Batman in real life. As such, it will fire the imagination with possibilities hitherto considered beyond what reality allows. Be warned though, that it isn't a fluff book; this is a serious read full of actual science and medical fact. Still, you really need to take a look.

APPENDIX "A": EXAMPLE LIST OF NECESSARY ITEMS FOR THE CRIME-FIGHTING SUPERHERO

First Aid:

- Gauze and Sterile pads
- Bandages of multiple types, and slings
- Band-Aids of all types, along with antibiotic cream
- Complete suturing kit (needles, thread, etc.)
- Supplies for making plaster casts in case of broken bones
- QuikClot to stop bleeding from wounds
- Alcohol, peroxide, and iodine
- Medical grade cyanoacrylate glue

Weaponry:

- Knives, swords, axes and machetes
- Long-guns, handguns, shotguns and ammo for all (probably need reloading equipment too)
- Smokeless and black powder (gunpowder); cannon fuse too
- Batons (extendable and solid), Baseball bats, saps/blackjacks
- Tasers and pepper spray
- Sap gloves and/or brass/titanium/G-10/carbon fiber knuckles
- Kubotan or other keychain weapon

Body Armour:

- Kevlar or spectra level 3A or level 4
- Plate carrier with various plates to suit different missions
- Chain mail (vest, shirt, head covering, gloves)
- Polycarbonate anti-stab vest
- Ballistic face mask and matching helmet
- Some form of leg and arm armour
- Cut-resistant gloves (could be hard-knuckle version)

Costume/Uniform /Disguise:

- Masks (soft or hard, possibly both)
- Silicone masks and matching sleeves
- Full movie make-up kit (take some lessons to learn its use)
- Cloak, cape or trench coat
- Utility belt and/or cargo pants
- Appropriate footwear for the mission and your hero type
- Coloured contact lenses

Necessary Drugs:

- Narcotics (Percocet, hydrocodone, morphine, Demerol, Tylenol 3, etc.)
- Antihistamines (Benadryl is about the best)
- Other pain killers (Tylenol, Tylenol 1, Ibuprofen, naproxen)
- Steroids (Anavar, Deca-Durabolin, etc.)
- Ephedrine (to get that "WOO, time to fight crime!" boost; also a decongestant)
- Antispasmodic muscle relaxers (Cyclobenzaprine, valium, clonazepam, etc.)
- Antibiotics, many varieties

Surveillance:

- Night vision goggles or monocular
- Binoculars and a telescope
- Hunting cameras with large memory capacity
- "Pinhole" cameras
- Directional microphone
- Video recording glasses and lapel pin camera

Miscellaneous:

- Shark repellant
- Bug repellant (probably required more often than the stuff for sharks)

- Various lengths and diameters of rope; rappelling gear as well
- Butane torch lighter and butane to refill it
- Ferro rod and striker
- Compass and a GPS
- Smart phone (have the power of a computer on the go)
- Pens, notepads and pencils
- Set of two-way radios if operating as part of a team
- Protein powder, vitamins and mineral supplements
- Duct tape and handcuffs
- Saw, blowtorch, and assorted hand tools
- Bike, car, skateboard or other means of transportation

APPENDIX "B": REINVENTING YOURSELF...A PICTORIAL EXERCISE

Visualization exercises are a mainstay of self-help groups, motivational seminars, and other assorted whack-jobs...however, they are also employed by elite athletes who perform amazing physical feats seemingly beyond human capacity. Whether it's top Olympic athletes, MMA champions or basketball stars rolling in huge piles of cash, they all use the power of visualization to achieve their goals.

But not any old visualization will do; you must picture yourself at the pinnacle of achievement, strong, confident, unbeatable. Furthermore, it must be task/goal-specific; picturing oneself as an elite football player will not help out when the mission involves storming a drug-lord's fortress while encased in armour and festooned with weaponry (it might seem obvious, but you'd be surprised at how many people go about it all wrong...). So, what do **you** want to be? What are **your** goals?

Well, *obviously* you want to be a violent vigilante superhero, imposing your mighty vision of Justice upon the world! If not, you wouldn't have bought this book...and if you mistakenly did, your feeble, sheep-like brain would have been overwhelmed along the way, leaving you curled in the corner making "meep, meep" noises. You aren't making "meep, meep" noises, are you? No? Good for you; let's continue.

Okay, so you need to fully immerse yourself in the heroic milieu, and the coolest way to do that is through comic-book style mythology and imagery. So first, you're going to find a cool location that has the correct atmosphere to it, you know, a place that just *clicks* in the depths of your soul. You'll know it when you find it; you may feel a sense of dislocation or euphoria...this is good, and confirms that the next step into a wilder, weirder world can commence. Now, assume the most heroic, appropriate pose possible, and take a picture:

Good, you should be feeling pretty fucking awesome right now; if not, repeat until you feel pretty fucking awesome.

Next, print off the picture on a full-size sheet of paper; black and white is fine, and may be more effective (it's up to you...take some initiative for fuck's sake!). Now, take a dark, soft pencil (2B at minimum, charcoal might be better) and blacken the back of the picture entirely.

Tape a clean sheet of paper to a table, then tape the picture with blackened back right on top of it. Tape it securely. Then, take a ball-point pen and go over all the areas and features that stand out best to you...really work them over.

In the next picture here, you'll see the top sheet being peeled back, exposing the sheet below (and showing the blackened back portion). You can see how the image has been transferred to the previously pristine paper:

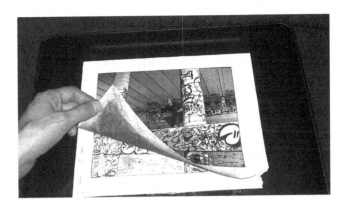

All right, you're into the home stretch now! Simply go over all the spots you wish to pick out more, using a combination of black pen and pencils. Smudging penciled-in areas with your finger can help give better shadow effects...but don't worry, as you're going for comic-book rather than replicating the Mona Lisa. If you have even a tiny bit of talent (or perseverance), the end result should look something like this:

Well shit, that looks not half bad, eh? I've certainly seen worse drawing for sale on the shelves. ☺

Use the finished product as a meditation focal point, or laminate it and use it as a placemat at the table. If the inspirational potency begins to fade, go on quests to find other locations that embody the characteristics and atmosphere you seek. Doing it more than once is actually recommended, as research shows that the brain becomes more fully engaged when we manually transmit images and words rather than passively accepting, or merely contemplating them. Over time, you will find that it takes less effort to get into the "heroic mindset"; you'll already be there!